Independently

Copyright L. Richmond 2024

L. Richmond asserts the moral right to be identified as the author of this work.

https://bio.site/LouiseRichmondAuthor

This novel is entirely a work of fiction. The names, characters and incidents portrayed in it are the work of the authors imagination. Any resemblance to actual persons, living or dead, events is entirely coincidental.

All rights reserved. No part of this publication may be reproduced, stored in a retrieval system, or transmitted, in any form or by any means, electronic, mechanical, photocopy, recording or otherwise, without prior permission from the author.

A.Livingstone asserts the moral right to be identified as the artist of the cover art.

Find more of A. Livingstone's art @TheGlitteringFox

Dear Kelly,

The House on Upper Float Road

Louise Richmond

This is a perfectly, imperfect proof copy. Let is remind you that we do not need to be the 'perfect' version of ourself to 'show up'.

Keep going, the world needs you, just as you are.

Louise
X

Chapter One

34 years ago

"I remember my 7th birthday. Mum and Dad had bought me a Cindy doll, and I thought she was the bee's knees. I was so happy. I would brush her hair, dress her, give her baths."
Elizabeth and Ian were reminiscing about their childhoods. They were both born in the early 1960s. They had recently become parents to a beautiful, healthy baby girl weighing exactly 8 lbs. They had called her Jess Elizabeth Rose. Jess after Ian's mother. Elizabeth after Elizabeth. Rose after Elizabeth's mother. Elizabeth couldn't quite believe that this tiny baby was hers. Jess was Elizabeth's first biological family member as she was adopted. Some days Elizabeth thought there was a clear resemblance to herself and other days she could see Ian.
"Oh, a space hopper for me. I remember trying to hop down the steep hill and it taking off, me holding on to it. You can still get those. We'll get her one when she's old enough," said Ian.
They both laughed looking at their sleeping ten-month-old baby girl. Who'd have thought that just a few hours later Elizabeth would take her own life.

***

The dust. The cracks. The creaking floorboards. Jess sat on the floor amongst the dust and the cobwebs, too tired to care if her clothes became dirty from sitting there.

It was still daylight outside, but the room was not well-lit, with dirty windows and no electric. How was she supposed to sell this one?

She knew what was expected of her: a work of fiction based on loose facts. 33 Upper Float Road, a comfortable 1930s three-bedroom semi-detached home with the potential to be a stunning property. Ideal for first-time buyers looking to put their own stamp on the place. The thing was, she now felt like this grey area of marketing properties was just an outright lie. The truth was that this was a cobweb-infested house situated in the highest, coldest village in England, with the main gable falling apart and in desperate need of a heating system that the landlord never bothered to install for the old lady who lived here and died alone three months ago. Poor old Maggie, living here alone with no heating, no water, no electricity. The kitchen had a tiny sink and a single hob stove on top of a cramped kitchen counter. Jess wondered what had happened to Maggie in her life to end up alone. Was she happy here, living a simple life with no need or desire to spend money on house renovations? Or was it the opposite? Was she broke, cold and unhappy here?

It was December when Jess arrived at the property and found a pile of mail behind the door. Mostly bills and final reminders. Even the dead were expected to pay their bills on time. Jess figured Maggie had left no one behind to cancel them for her. As she picked up the letters out of the way of the entrance, she found a handwritten card addressed to Miss Maggie Wright.

She knew it was a Christmas card as she could see baby Jesus in a manger behind the thin white envelope. Now sitting on the floor in her ankle-length plum puffy winter coat with her white scarf covering her face, taming in the wayward strands of her black curly hair, she held the envelope in her hand.

Would it be wrong to open it? She pondered. It would probably end up in a skip if she didn't open it. There might be a return address. She could let the sender of the card know the sad news of Maggie's passing, or else they may keep sending cards year after year, believing she was still alive.

Jess felt sad that Maggie was dead, and the sender didn't seem to care enough to be in touch regularly or visit. On the other hand, Jess wondered if it was comforting to think that a dear old friend, perhaps ageing, unwell, or living far away, still took the time to send Maggie a Christmas card.

***

Back in the day, Jess had been the top seller at Move It for three years in a row. However, she had lost any passion she had for her career years ago. Lately, she had just been going through the

motions, and her mood was sometimes flat. She was trying hard to take care of herself, eating right, exercising, and going to bed early. Sometimes this all seemed to help, and at other times, it didn't seem to make any difference to her energy levels or frame of mind.
For 33 Upper Float Road, she would have to schedule viewings in the daytime due to the lack of electricity and workable plumbing. Her thoughts returned to dear old Maggie living here alone.
She opened the envelope. Yes, just as she had expected, there was baby Jesus, lying in a straw-filled manger with a golden halo above his head. Inside, it read:

Dear Maggie,

I hope this card finds you well.

Betty and I are still here in the Yorkshire Dales, though we haven't had a walk down to the stream for a while as we are not as mobile as we once were.

Happy Christmas.

Best wishes, love from Alice xxx

Jess wiped a tear away from her eye. There was no return address, but her second scenario of a well-meaning old friend had warmed her heart. She decided to take the card home and place it among her own Christmas cards.

She stood up and brushed off her coat to remove the dust. Then, she made a note of her valuation figure to go along with the pictures she had taken. Since this was her last job of the day, it was finally time to go home.

She had intended to stop at the supermarket on the way home to pick up the ingredients for a homemade spaghetti bolognaise, but now she could not find the energy to be bothered. She knew Benjamin would not be home anyway so she would resort to the cheese and crackers which she always had to hand.

She put the Christmas card in her pocket before making a final check of the property and locking it up. As she headed to her car, she looked back for a moment. It could be a lovely little home for somebody, , she thought. But it really did need a lot of work.

As Jess entered her own house, she switched on the light. It was completely dark outside now and cold inside. Benjamin had probably gone straight from work to the indoor ski slopes at Castleford.

She switched the heating on, wondering how much an hour would cost. She boiled the kettle and watched the smart meter notch up the charges. Looking at her own fully functioning kitchen, she imagined Maggie making herself a cuppa, boiling her whistling kettle on her single-hob gas stove.

Jess took her cheese and crackers, cup of tea and hot water bottle into the cosy living room, placing them down on the side table while she stood Maggie's Christmas card up with the others. Baby Jesus looked back at her from his improvised cradle.

She thought about telling Benjamin about the property and the card, but she would leave for work in the morning before he was out of bed so she wouldn't get the opportunity. He wouldn't notice it. He never looked at the Christmas cards they received and didn't write any or sign his name on the cards they sent out together. He left that to Jess.

Jess flicked through the TV channels. Something Christmassy, perhaps? No. A documentary on serial killers? Maybe. A reality TV series? Nope. A film? Possibly. By the time she had finished flicking through the options, half an hour had passed, and she decided not to watch anything. Tired, she went up to bed.

In the stillness of her room, she was left with her thoughts. She would have liked to share them with someone. Maybe I should think of getting a pet to talk to, she pondered. A cat, maybe. A dog couldn't be left while she was at work. A tabby cat.

She thought of Maggie, Betty and Alice, a trio of best friends who had many adventures over the years.

She invented a story. Maggie was a world-famous female climber. Betty was the strongest woman in the world, and Alice was their manager. She laughed at herself, but she wanted to imagine them having full and exciting lives. It would make today seem less sad.

Night-time was both Jess' best and worst time of the day. It was when she did not have to be perceived. She was alone and in no one else's view. She didn't have a reflection on anyone. She didn't have an imposed expectation on her. She could get comfortable and warm. No one was looking at her or judging her. She could finally relax, breathe, be herself, feeling a deep sense of relief that only the night could bring.

It was, however, too short a time. It felt like trying to keep hold of the tiniest grains of sand as they slipped through her fingers. It was never enough. She wanted more of this quiet moment of the day. The peacefulness in the time before bed always passed too quickly. Unlike the rest of her day. But she also felt lonely. She wanted someone to share her comfortable place, to accept her. Gentle company, she liked to call it. Someone who wouldn't try to change her or criticise her. Someone who wouldn't demand anything. Just be there. Listening. Supporting.

Getting into bed also meant that when she woke, tomorrow would be here. She was not ready for tomorrow; she was still recovering from today. She was so tired, but she didn't want to go to sleep yet and miss this golden hour.

Eventually, she drifted off into a deep sleep. As predicted, she didn't hear Benjamin come home and get into bed next to her, and he was undisturbed by her as she got up for work and left him there sleeping.

It was lunchtime, and Jess was hungry because of last night's meagre tea of cheese and crackers and that she'd opted for an extra twenty minutes in bed over having time for breakfast.

After a busy morning, she had a break before her afternoon appointments. Even though it was winter, the sun was shining and there was no wind or rain. She decided to have an alfresco lunch and bought a sandwich to eat in the local park.

She settled on a wooden bench that had seen better days and watched a bird circle in the air. She watched the occasional cloud flit past in the blue sky. She watched the bare trees swaying ever so slightly. She breathed in the cold, crisp air—a moment of tranquility in her hectic day.

The peace was broken by her phone ringing. It was the office.

"Hello," she answered, trying not to sound like she had a mouthful of sandwich.

"Hi, Jess." It was Praveen. "Sorry to interrupt your lunch break, but I just had an enquiry. Can you do a showing of 33 Upper Float Road at 5 pm today?"

"Yes, that's fine. Go ahead and put it in my diary," replied Jess.

"Great. Thanks, Jess. Enjoy your lunch," Praveen said and hung up.

Jess returned to her winter gazing for five more minutes as she finished her lunch, then set off to tackle her busy afternoon.

It was only midway into her second appointment that she had an awful thought. It would be nearly dark by 5 pm, and it was too late to cancel the appointment now. It would be too dark inside to show the property without light. What was she going to do?

She would just about have time to go home to fetch the three torches she kept in the garage. It was quite unconventional, but such at short notice, what else could she do?

***

"Hello, Mr Thomas and Miss Page. It's lovely to meet you. I'm Jess." They shook hands. They were a young couple in their early twenties, looking for their first property together.

"Nice to meet you," said the young man.

"Hello," said Miss Page, smiling.

"Just one thing before we enter the property," explained Jess. "It has no working utilities at the present moment, and as you can see, the sun is setting, so these torches will be useful." She smiled her biggest smile, forcing enthusiasm into her voice. The surprised couple took a torch each, and Jess led the way up the narrow driveway to the three stone steps to the front door.

Once inside, she continued, "The house has great potential for someone looking to put their own finish to a home. There is even an opportunity to decide your own layout downstairs, like fitting a bespoke kitchen. There are two rooms downstairs, a sitting room and a kitchen dining area."

The young couple appeared shell-shocked. They had not said a word since stepping inside the property, but Jess continued, "The property is currently vacant and therefore ready for a quick sale, no upward chain. There's a large garden out the back, which, of course, would be better appreciated in the light of day." She smiled again. "There are three bedrooms upstairs and a bathroom. If you'd like to go ahead and take a look?"

She pointed in the direction of the staircase.

"Be careful on the stairs in the dark," she called after them as they made their way up. Jess waited in the small front room. She jumped up and down on the spot to try and generate some body heat. It was so cold she could see her breath in the air. The old floorboards groaned under her feet.

It wasn't long until the pair returned.

"Thank you, erm, Jess, was it? I believe we have seen enough," said Mr Thomas.

"OK. Perhaps you'd like to arrange a viewing in the daylight?" Jess said, trying to be positive, but the couple were already on their way out the door. I'll take that as a no, she thought.

"Thank you for coming. Bye," she called after them.

When Jess got home, Benjamin was not there. He was supposed to be home; it was his turn to cook a meal. However, the house was in darkness, the heating was off, and the alarm was on. Standing in the entrance hall, she closed her eyes for a moment and imagined the house full of light, warmth and love, filling her heart with joy. She could smell delicious food coming from the kitchen and tried to guess what culinary masterpiece Benjamin was creating in there. She caught the scent of garlic, tomato, rosemary, and cheese; she could almost trick her senses into believing the smells were real as she salivated, and her tummy rumbled. He was making her favourite lasagne with garlic bread and Parmesan cheese. Her tummy rumbled again.

She shook herself, opened her eyes, took off her coat, untied her scarf and hung them by the door. She removed her boots, walked towards the kitchen, and closed her eyes again, imagining Benjamin singing their favourite song as he washed the pots in the sink. As she opened the door, he looked up and smiled at her.
"Right on time," he says to her. He enjoyed preparing a meal for them to share together because they are only happy when each other is happy. He knows how good it feels to come home to someone who loves you. Jess inhaled deeply, holding her breath and the image for just a moment. Then she exhaled, opening her eyes, and the image was gone.
Jess stood in darkness. The aromas disappeared, the joy seeped away, and the house was cold.

She didn't message Benjamin to ask where he was or when he'd be home. There seemed to be little point in doing so, as she would rather he didn't reply with some excuse that she'd heard a hundred times before. She was so tired of that predictable, disappointing routine.

Jess turned on the heating. She boiled the kettle and made a cup of Yorkshire tea, nice and milky, and toast with butter and jam. She took them into the living room and sat on the sofa, covering herself with a blanket until the house warmed. Not having the mental capacity to make any more decisions today, she switched on the TV and watched the first program that popped up on the home screen. It was a sci-fi detective show where the lead characters chase down a shape-shifting murderer. When it was over, Jess switched the heating off and went to bed.

The next morning, when she woke, Benjamin was beside her. He was fast asleep. Maybe he will be awake before I leave
 for work. Jess rekindled a fraction of hope for their fractured relationship. Her mind wandered, imagining them catching up over breakfast. Jess would put the kettle on, and Benjamin would get the milk from the fridge. He would then put the bread in the toaster while she put the milk back in the fridge and swapped it for the butter. They would be in perfect unison like a well-choreographed dance.

He would ask her what viewings she had today. She would ask him how many meetings he had. He would kiss her cheek while putting on his jacket. He would eat the last mouthful of toast and say, "I love you. See you tonight." She would reply, "I love you too. Have a good day."

It did not feel right to Jess. She knew they both had full-time jobs and separate hobbies, but should she really feel so lonely when she lived with her partner? She felt depleted and remembered how she used to try harder, putting all her efforts into the relationship. She would arrange date nights and special meals. She used to meet Benjamin for a quick walk at lunchtime when he knew he'd be working late into the evening.

It had all become one-sided though. Benjamin even started pushing back her suggestions, as if she was asking for too much by wanting to spend time with him. He would say things like, "It's out of my way," "I don't think I'll have time," or "I'm having lunch with some colleagues today." Once, when Jess had said she would make a special meal, his response had been quite brutal, like she had offered him his last meal before execution. "Why do you have to ask me that?" Benjamin had said. "You know I'm going to the slopes. Don't you want me to go? Why would you stop me from doing something I really want to do just to have a meal? We can do that anytime. Are you trying to start an argument?"

Not quite the response she had hoped for when asking her partner to share a nice home-cooked meal with her. So, slowly, over time, she'd stopped asking. She was in some kind of siege situation, and she didn't know how to escape. She started to feel like a stranger in her own home and starved of companionship. It wasn't the life she had imagined for herself.

***

The festive period had been relatively quiet for Jess. Her father and stepmother, on their retirement, had purchased a campervan — a classic 1967 VW T1 Split-Screen. It had always been their dream to own one and travel wherever they wanted. So, they sold their house and set off, planning their route as they went along. They had called her on Christmas Day from Lake Garda, Italy. It was 14 degrees and sunny. Jess was so happy for them and loved hearing all about their adventures. She often felt like she was living through their experiences these days.

She missed them both so much and often wished she could join them. Especially at this time of year when the days were short and starved of daylight. Jess and Benjamin spent Christmas Day together. It started pleasantly enough with them both on their best behaviour. They had a nice lie-in and a cup of tea in bed, which Jess made, and exchanged gifts. Jess overlooked that her gifts were not wrapped. She knew Benjamin had been busy with work up until Christmas Eve. She was just pleased he had remembered to get her something. After all, he only had one gift to buy, as she did the Christmas shopping for all their family and friends.

Later in the day, when it was time to eat the Christmas dinner Jess had prepared, she looked at the table with a smile. Even though it was just the two of them for Christmas this year, she had tried to make it feel special. She had dressed the table with mistletoe crackers and a Christmas candle, used the posh wine glasses and placed the linen napkins with their initials.

She called for Benjamin, who had been watching TV in the front room. He came into the kitchen and took his plate with no word of thanks, no smile, nothing. He just took the plate. Jess had used their best plates, the ones his mother had given as a housewarming present. Plate in hand, Benjamin walked past the beautifully laid-out table, returned to the sofa in front of the TV and started eating.

An unremarkable event. No argument. Jess didn't even feel cross. She just felt sad that Benjamin was so unaware or unappreciative of all the effort she had put into it. That on Christmas Day, when he was physically present, he was still somehow not, and she felt a void of loneliness. This was the exact moment she decided she did not fit into her own life anymore, and she did not feel loved. And it was in this moment that she decided to leave

Benjamin. Sitting alone at the table, she knew this would be her last Christmas dinner in this house with Benjamin. She poured herself a glass of red wine and felt the ghosts of all her Christmases past and the shadows dimming her unclear future. *Happy Christmas*, she thought as a single tear rolled down her cheek.

It was New Year's Eve. Jess was home alone. Benjamin had gone out with friends and would not be expected home. They had talked on Boxing Day. Jess had tried to explain how she could not go on in a lonely relationship that she had no hope of changing. She had done her best not to sound like she was portioning all the blame at Benjamin's feet. He could not give her what she needed, but maybe he had given her everything he could.

He was cross. That was his overriding emotional response. He was angry at her accusations. They were unjust and simply not true, he had insisted. But for Jess, Benjamin's reaction and his belief that there was no a problem was the problem. She was living a life that felt incredibly lonely, and she wanted someone to share her life –her thoughts , her hopes and dreams, her challenges and disappointments – to laugh with, to cry with. She needed that companionship. She found it strange that they were living as partners, but their realities were so different. If she had any doubts about ending the relationship, Benjamin's anger and defensiveness confirmed her decision that the relationship had to end.

Chapter Two

The next morning, on New Year's Day, Jess woke alone. She questioned her sanity on a decision about a thought she had been ruminating on for the past week. Today was a Bank Holiday, but tomorrow, she would be back at work, and she would start the process. She was going to buy 33 Upper Float Street. It would be her new home. She liked the house; it was a good fit. So, it was depressed, rundown and falling apart., but she needed new start; she would make the journey of recovery with the house. They would rebuild each other.

***

33 Upper Float Street now had electricity and running water. Jess moved in three weeks ago, at the beginning of February. The process had only taken five weeks, and her professional knowledge and contacts helping the process run smoothly. For the moment, in the bathroom, she had to make do with a sink and cold water With Where the kitchen would be, a small fridge stood on the floor thick with crumbled plaster, and a microwave and kettle sat on top of a fold-out garden table. Her tiny fridge could just about hold the basics: cheese, a bottle of milk and some butter. If she needed running water, she had to go upstairs.

The gable end had been secured to prevent it from falling away. Today, the building inspector was coming to check the work and sign it off, so the floorboards had to be lifted on the landing and in the smallest bedroom above the stairs.

Looking around Jesse's new home, it didn't seem like much had been done, but she was making the foundations strong. There's no point papering over the cracks, she thought to herself. Although, with this house, the cracks were huge chasms, so papering over them had never been an option anyway. And Jess, like her home, was beginning to rebuild herself from the ground up.

Jess had decided to keep a wardrobe that Maggie had left behind. It was in her spare room, which she planned to fix up for her dad and step-mum when they were home visiting from their travels. The wardrobe was handcrafted from a dark, solid wood. All it needed was some sanding and polish with wood wax, and it would look great as a nice feature in the room.

Jess removed the wardrobe doors from their hinges. Inside was a built-in set of drawers. Jess removed the top drawer and set it to one side. As she repeated the process, she came across a fabric-bound book in the second drawer. Her heart leapt. it. She was instantly intrigued because she knew she had found something special. But what was written in it?

Jess picked up the book and blew away the dust. The floral book jacket appeared hand-sewn, fitting snuggly around the book as if it was purpose made. She ran her hand over the top of the book trying to discover what maybe inside, like a clairvoyant trying to get messages from beyond the grave.

Finally, she turned the cover and the words 'Private ~ Maggie's Diary' were written inside. *Jess smiled. Maggie's private diary!* She shouldn't look, but now, living here in Maggie's house, she felt like it was okay to see what was written on those pages, as if she was a custodian of Maggie's things. In fact, she reassured herself, if she *didn't* look, Maggie may as well be forgotten. And honestly, it was a welcome distraction from her own life.

As Jess turned the first page, she was about to learn more about Maggie than she could have ever imagined.

A knock at the door made Jess jump to her feet. It was the building inspector. She carefully placed the diary back in the last drawer still to be emptied and went to answer the door.

The inspector was a tall man of few words. He wore his ID badge clipped to his shirt and carried a clipboard and pen. Jess followed him upstairs as he looked through the holes in the floor to check the metal ties were all in place. He chewed the end of his pen and "hmmm-ed" a lot. Thankfully, after less than ten minutes, he looked up and signed the paper on his clipboard. Peering at Jess over the top of his glasses, he said, "Yes, that's all fine." He handed her the piece of paper and left. Jess carefully filed it away with all the other paperwork for the house and immediately returned upstairs to retrieve the diary. She sat cross-legged on the floor and began to read.

Maggie's Diary

20 May 1960

I went out with Alice and Betty today. We met by the stream like we usually do. We took our shoes and socks off and paddled in the water. It was nice to be outside on such a bright day. It lifted my mood. Alice squeezed my hand and asked if I was okay. I smiled and nodded. I'm so glad I have friends like Alice and Betty. Betty was dancing in the water, splashing her feet and wiggling her hips. She was singing 'Cathy's Clown', so me and Alice joined in.
Don't want your loooove. Don't want your kiiiiisses anymore. I die each time. I hear this sound. Here he cooooomes, that's Cathy's clown.
We all sang together and danced in the shallow water. Thank God for moments like this. For the glimmers of joy in my life. For my friends. We have made plans to go to the cinema tomorrow night to see *The Challenge* starring Anthony Quayle.

Jess could not believe what she had stumbled upon. After finding the Christmas card, she had created an image of Maggie, Alice and Betty, and now she had a direct window into their real lives. It seemed as if it was meant for her. Jess felt a sense of purpose she hadn't felt in a long time. Even though she lived alone, she felt less lonely knowing she had the house and Maggie's company through her diary entries.

Living in Maggie's world was exciting and engaging, and Jess became even more invested in repairing the house.

Jess decided that she would reward herself by reading more of Maggie's diary whenever she had finished another task in the house. Now that the gable end inspection was done, she would return to the wardrobe. She removed the last drawer and placed the diary on the bedside table in her own bedroom safekeeping.

As she began sanding the old wardrobe, she found her mind was no longer overwhelmed by replaying her break-up with Benjamin and she felt all the sadness dissipate. Instead, her thoughts turned to Maggie. Wondering how much she could learn about her life from the diary. She couldn't wait to read the next entry.

25 May 1960

After a lovely weekend at the cinema and spending time with Alice and Betty, my thoughts have returned to darker matters. I can barely bring myself to write about it, let alone say it out loud. Only Alice knows my secret; she's kept it from

Betty. I don't want to dwell on it. I don't want to acknowledge it. I have time.

Jess had to keep reading. She was now so invested in Maggie. Living here at 33 Upper Float Road and finding the diary. What was Maggie's secret?

1 June 1960

I was up early this morning to work at the shop. Usually, I get so tired, like I'm walking around in a fog, but today, I was okay. Alice was waiting for me when I'd finished. She keeps asking me what I'm going to do, but I honestly don't know. She took all my dresses and a couple of skirts for me to alter them. She's a great seamstress. At least I'll have something to wear. I know that to get pregnant out of wedlock is shameful. Mum and Dad will say I've shamed them and almost certainly make me give the baby up. I don't want them to take my baby.

Maggie was pregnant. It was hard for Jess to stop reading there, but she still had so much work to do on the house. She decided to use it as motivation. As soon as she finished painting the hallway, she would continue reading. She distracted herself, listening to music from the '60s.

4 June 1960

It's been so awful. My mum knows about the baby. She had noticed I'd not been using the cloth pads and began questioning me. When I finally told her, she asked if I could get married. I told her no. She said there was no way I can keep the baby That her only child could do this to her and be such a disappointment. She said I would have to go to a mother and baby home.
I'd be a better mother than she is. I want to keep the baby, but without my parents' support, how can I afford to? On my shop worker wage? And will I still have a job after the birth?

***

Jess was making good progress with the house, and Benjamin finally decided he would stay in their old home and buy Jess out. She was happy with this decision even though she knew they could have made more selling it on the open market. He would buy her out, and then she could afford a kitchen.

11 July 1960

I overheard Mother and Father talking late last night. They are finalising and rehearsing my 'cover' story for when they send me away to have the baby. The have finally agreed to tell everyone that I've been invited to attend a school for young women for an extended period, where I will further my education and learn secretarial skills.

It all sounded very far-fetched to me. I've never expressed an interest in learning secretarial or typing skills. I've begged and pleaded with them not to send me. I've considered running away, but where would I go?

Jess felt a sense of relief as the paperwork was finalized, and she would soon receive the funds from Benjamin. Once she had the money, she could hire tradespeople to help her. Throughout the process, Jess and Benjamin communicated through solicitors, as Benjamin was still very angry with her and had no intention of speaking to her again. To Benjamin, she was very much the villain in the story. Nevertheless, if it put an end to the situation with Benjamin and work could begin on her kitchen, it would all be worth it. She continued the decorating and then went back to reading. She couldn't believe that Maggie's parents were planning to send her away.

23 September 1960

My beautiful Nancy was born today. She's perfect. I was allowed to hold her and take care of her. Her adoptive parents haven't come for her yet. I hope they never come, and she stays with me forever. Most other girls here at St. Boniface Mother and Baby Home had their babies with them for five or six weeks.

The nuns keep telling me it's for the best. But it's not best for me. How can they be allowed to do this? The nuns tell me I sinned, and I could atone by giving my baby to a loving couple who needed a child. To not do so would be selfish, and this is the only way I can make things right. That's what they teach here. It's as if all they care about is finding babies for the parents on their list; there's no care for the girls. One girl who has just left is only 15– a child herself.

Jess did not have children, she had not reached a point where she could reconcile the adult she had become with the idea of being a parent. She was turning 35 on her next birthday and had just ended her relationship with Benjamin, but it was more than that. She was highly functioning and successful in her career, but she lived with chronic and unpredictable anxiety. She had concluded that having a child would be the most anxiety-inducing thing one could do. It would be like having a piece of your heart walk around outside of your body. She had convinced herself it would be best not to have a child. Looking at the situation with hindsight, she may have felt that Benjamin would not be able to provide the rock steady emotional support she would need.
She had yet to get around to decorating her bedroom. The walls had pink florals on the top half and pink stripes on the bottom, separated by a striped border. The paper was peeling from the corners and was damp and mouldy by the

window. The room had bare floorboards and badly needed insulation and decoration.

Jess drifted off to sleep with ease and began to dream. In her dream, she was standing at the bow of a small ship, gazing out at the endless ocean. As the ship cut through the water, she felt a gentle breeze blew on her face and closed her eyes to take a deep breath. She felt calm. When she opened her eyes again, she could see land coming into view. Suddenly, the wind picked up, the sky darkened, and the waves grew. Jess panicked as she was thrown off balance, reaching out to a rail to steady herself. She moved forward, gripping the rail until she reached the ship's bow.

At that moment, she realised she was on the only person on the ship, with no crew or passengers. She froze, gripping the rail tight with both hands. She found herself in control of the ship as it sped toward land. Now, the waves were crashing over onto the deck, drenching her. She cried for help, knowing that no one would hear her. She screamed.

Suddenly, Jess was awake, her heart racing as her mind tried to piece together what was happening. She finally remembered the dream, and her body began to settle. Although Jess was exhausted, she was not ready to return to the land of nod just yet. She turned on her bedside light and reached for Maggie's diary.

11 October 1960

I held Nancy for the last time today. I held her so tight. They said her mum and dad were here to collect her, but that's not true. I'm her mummy. I always will be. I wanted to run after the nurse who took her. I wanted to shout, "She's mine, don't take her." But where would I go? Where could I take her? Mum and Dad said I could only come home if I gave up Nancy and never talked about her again. I've nowhere else to go. I am defeated and broken. It's a nightmare. It's not real, it can't be real. I cry all the time, and the nuns say it's just baby blues.

Jess felt heartbroken for Maggie as tears ran down her face. She couldn't believe what she was reading; this was someone's life, Maggie's life. Her daughter had been taken away from her. Despite the heartache, she continued reading.

15 October 1960

They're sending me home today, home to my parents, but now I'm returning as a mother to a daughter, just like my own mum. But I won't be bringing my baby girl with me. I'm not sure if I shall ever see her again. I'm expected to go home like nothing has changed. Everything has changed. My whole world has changed. My whole body has changed. My tummy still looks like my baby is inside. I sometimes cradle it and pretend to talk to Nancy inside. My milk is still here in my breast, ready to feed her. I've cried so much since they took her, but only quietly at night. If we girls cry in front of the nuns, they have little or no sympathy and even call us names.

My relationship with my parents has changed forever. Would my mother have given me up if she and Dad had not been married? If Mum and Dad really loved me, they would have kept me no matter what and, therefore, know why I desperately want my baby. But I know it's too late now. I am defeated and worried that I may never see my Nancy again. The whole world is upside down.

For the next few weeks, Jess worked hard day and night, dedicating herself to her full-time job and her responsibilities at home, while also finding time to follow Maggie's journey in her free moments. This busy schedule left her no time to think about being single or about Benjamin.

Jess had discovered that Maggie had no choice but to return home after giving birth to Nancy. Her relationship with her parents became strained because they pretended that the pregnancy and birth had never happened and denied the existence of their granddaughter. There was constantly an elephant in the room, the biggest one you have ever seen, yet her father and mother looked through it as if it were a ghost.

After reading Maggie's diary, thoughts of motherhood stirred within Jess. It had always been a possibility for her, but the time was never right. Perhaps when the stars and the heavens aligned, when she had discovered the right concoction of vitamins and minerals to 'fix' her, or when she had met the right partner. However, none of these things had happened, and now she was reaching an age where she would be referred to as a geriatric mother in pregnancy medical terms.

Maybe I should freeze my eggs, she considered. But it didn't feel like an option. Everything that needed to change to make her consider motherhood seemed impossible. But reading about Maggie and the bond she had developed when giving birth to Nancy and how desperate she was to keep her made her reconsider. The journey into motherhood had physically and mentally changed Maggie. The Maggie who had returned home to her parents' house was not the same as the one that had left. Even without her baby, she was now a mother.

Jess suddenly felt ill. She must have eaten something that didn't agree with her. Despite feeling exhausted, she had pushed herself to work on the house renovations. Today, she had managed a full day at work but went straight to bed when she got home. As she lay there, she realised she hadn't had her period. She always felt ill before her period was due, more irritable and tired. She often felt sick, and her anxiety would ramp up. Jess eventually closed her eyes and slept for ten hours.

She didn't feel refreshed in the morning though. She was as tired as ever, dragging her bones out of bed. She forced herself through another day, eating nothing, only to return to bed as soon as possible.

She rang in sick the next morning, but at least she had finally started her period. She was bleeding lightly, not like her usual heavy periods. She made herself a hot water bottle and a cup of tea and curled up in bed with Maggie's diary.

3 November 1960.

It's my birthday today. I'm 21. Mum and Dad bought me a bracelet. I smiled and said thank you, trying to be polite. But inside, I still feel so angry with them. I'm their daughter, and they want to spend my birthday with me, but where is *my* daughter? Where is Nancy? I get so cross sometimes, but if I show it, Mum and Dad get cross back. They won't acknowledge that I'm a mother too now. They say it's not the same. Then they try and control my every movement. So, I hold my tongue. Sometimes, this rage of frustration boils within me. It needs to escape, get out, and be released. I took the small knife from the cutlery drawer in the kitchen and held it on my arm. I gripped the handle so tight and thought I might slice the skin to let all the anger and pain out of my body. Then I let the knife go. It had left a tiny nick on my forearm, something and nothing, but I watched a small drop of blood trickle down, and it distracted me. I dampened a cloth and bathed it. I fixed it because I could. I could see the problem, and I could fix it. It was within my control, so little else is these days.

I am now the magical age of Twenty-one, young and free, my whole life ahead of me. So why do I feel like my life is over? But it's okay. I've got really good at playing the "I'm not a mother. I'm just a daughter role."

Jess rallied herself for the next day and made her way to work. She was showing an unusual property – an old forge converted into a beautiful, unique cottage on the hillside. It was on two levels with the upstairs at ground level on one side. The old forge entrance created a splendid feature at the basement level. The garden would be beautiful in the spring, the garden would be beautiful with its abundant shrubbery and shaded seating. Inside, on the second floor, was a large kitchen/diner leading to a cosy front room with a real open fire. At the basement level were three bedrooms and a family bathroom. Jess spent the best part of the day there. She had six separate showings and was confident it would sell quickly.

Jess's period symptoms had eased to just a few days of light bleeding, although she still felt a little tired. She put that down to the stress of the break-up, the move and all the physical work of the house renovations. She had experienced so many changes in her life during the last month; it was no wonder it had taken its toll on her body. Mentally, she felt better. She was sleeping better too, managing to get eleven hours each night. For the past two nights, she had gone to bed at 8.30 pm and hadn't stirred until 7.30 am. She needed her rest because today she had three second showings of the old forge.

23 November 1960.

I've mainly been spending my time at work. The more money I earn, the more independent I will be. Today, one of Mum and Dad's friends came into the shop and expressed surprise at seeing me, assuming that I would have taken up secretarial work by now after my mother and father had had me educated. I was livid. Through gritted teeth, I told them that I preferred my current job but thanked them for inquiring. I'll be saving forever to move out into my own place, but I will get there eventually. I'm determined. I haven't been out with Alice and Betty since I got home; I am saving my money. Alice is meeting me today for a walk after work to catch up.
I am looking forward to seeing her, but it's like going back to a time before Nancy didn't exist. How will it make me feel? At least I can talk to her about Nancy without being silenced.

Chapter Three

Jess sat on the edge of her new bath. The floor was bare, but the tiling was finished – creamy white tiles with a border of turquoise. She checked the time on her phone again. It wasn't time yet.

24 November 1960

It was wonderful to see Alice. She gave me the biggest hug and held me while I sobbed. It was a relief to be able to let everything out. She knew she couldn't fix things for me or get Nancy back but held space for me to feel my pain. Afterward, we just walked and talked. She even brought me a bag of my favourite dolly mixtures. When I was done crying, she filled me in everything I'd missed while I'd been away.

Jess checked her phone again; it was time now. This moment could change her whole life. She looked. Positive. She was not going to believe one test, so she opened the second one she had purchased. She waited, and again, the positive result came. Jess was pregnant.
She sat on the edge of the bath, staring at the positive tests, holding one in each hand. She felt something she wasn't expecting to feel – excitement. It came alongside a package of

emotions: terror, confusion, loneliness, and disbelief. But there, in the centre of it all, was undeniable excitement. There were so many emotions to unpack, and so much she would eventually have to face, like telling Benjamin. But for tonight, it would be her secret. She would make herself something nice to eat and then go to bed early to read Maggie's diary until she drifted off to sleep.

21 December 1960

I hate them all. I became so cross with my mother today it was like I was possessed. Every time she raised her voice, it was as if I were being attacked and provoked into a rage. She said I must tell Aunt Ada when she visits on Christmas Day that I was away at secretarial school for a few months earlier this year, and if she asked for details, I should say it was on the east coast near Scarborough. I could feel my blood boiling. I snapped. I growled at her like a wild animal. I moved towards the counter and swiped my arm across it, sending her favourite teapot, two china cups and their saucers smashing against the wall. I waited for her reaction, but she didn't say anything. I think she had been stunned into silence. I glared at her, feeling tense and angry. I ran out of the front door, leaving it wide open. I ran across the fields until I finally stopped at the stream. I had to catch my breath. I collapsed on my hands and knees, panting. When darkness fell, I walked back across the field into the village. I was shivering. There was a bitter ice wind, the kind that ushers in a snowfall. In my rage, I had not stopped to put on a coat. I needed to get warm but didn't want to go home.

I stood outside the tearoom and counted the coins in my cardigan pocket to see if I had tuppence for a cup of tea, and that's when I met Susan. She had kind, pretty, green eyes and a friendly smile, about 30 years of age. She invited me to have a warm drink with her. She agreed it felt cold enough for snow.

We went inside and sat at the table near the window and talked for an hour. I'd never seen her before, and she said she was just passing through to pick up supplies.

She told me she had left home when she was about my age. She whispered to me that she'd gotten pregnant at my age and had been forced to give away her baby. I couldn't believe it.

Strangely, I feel as if I've known her all my life. I'm meeting her again tomorrow.

Jess loved spring. After opening the curtains, she stood at her bedroom window for a moment, closed her eyes and faced the sun. She had her first ultrasound scan a couple of weeks ago and everything was looking fine. Today, she would finish decorating her bedroom today so that the paint would be dry before the carpet fitters came next week. First though, she would go for a stroll in the sunshine to watch the lambs skipping around the farm fields.

22 December 1960

I woke early to leave the house and meet Susan before Mum and Dad woke. She was waiting for me by the gate leading to the field. Together, we walked down to the stream, talking all the way. I told her about Nancy. She stopped and held onto my arms, telling me how sorry she was and how she understood. She told me how lucky she had been to become a mother to her little boy a few years later and to be able to live independently. She moved in with a commune of like-minded people who all worked and lived together. She still lives there and has invited me to join her. The commune is about an hour's drive away in Starbotton, just far enough away from my parents. Susan said I would be allowed to be a grieving mother and talk about Nancy there. I would have my own room and food provided in exchange for work. Susan also said she knows someone who might even be able to get a photograph of Nancy for me. She's leaving tomorrow, and I've decided to go with her. I don't plan to tell anyone, not even Alice, because I don't want Mum and Dad to find me.

Now, 33 Upper Float Road had a fully functional modern kitchen/diner with patio doors that looked out onto the manicured lawn with an amazing display of flowers blooming at the start of spring. Jess could only take credit for cutting the grass; the flowers were all Maggie's work. Jess pictured Maggie enjoying her beautiful garden and tending the flowers. Perhaps she was happy here after all, having clearly put a lot of care and attention into this garden.

Jess was enjoying this long summer solstice day, the longest day of the year. She now knew she was having a little girl and would start decorating the nursery, the smallest of the three bedrooms. She knew her little girl would be in her room for a while, but she wanted the house finished and all the paint fumes and chaos of house renovation gone before the baby arrived.

24 December 1960

Today, I left Ingleton. I left everyone and everything behind, but I don't feel sad. In truth, I'd already left everything that was mine behind the day they took Nancy from me.

Susan picked me up in her red Ford Falcon. The drive took just over an hour, but it felt like minutes as I was so engaged in our conversation. Susan is so easy to talk to. She just gets it. She doesn't shut me down. I can talk about Nancy and being a mother – a mother without her baby.

My room is next to hers. She wanted me to feel safe and welcome. There are about a dozen small bungalows, most with three bedrooms. Susan and I will share with Bee whom I will meet in the morning before a tour of the communal areas. Tomorrow is Christmas Day. Susan says the whole community will gather to share a meal in the afternoon, allowing me to meet everyone else.

Jess learnt that Maggie seemed very happy in her new home. When she had attended the Christmas meal and other community events, members had showered her with praise and admiration for dealing with the separation from her child and having the strength and foresight to leave her parents' home. Susan had raised Maggie's hopes that her contact had obtained a picture of Nancy and that it would arrive very soon.

Jess was worried as she read, though, as Maggie was in a vulnerable state. She hoped these people Maggie had stumbled upon were genuine.

Jess had studied psychology at school and remembered how cult members "love-bomb" new recruits, aiming to create a positive association in their minds between them by offering something the 'recruit' longed for. In Maggie's case, she longed for recognition as a mother and an acknowledgement of her daughter's existence. While it may not have been a cult, it was presented to Maggie as an "intentional" commune where people pooled resources and agreed to live a certain way. Membership was closed, and residents had to be selected and committed to the commune's purpose by agreeing to live by rules determined by the group leader.

They called themselves The Bright Light Living Commune and sold themselves as built on three fundamental principles: trust, community, and sharing– not much room for personal space or individual thinking , Jess reflected.

Maggie mentioned in her diary that during a community event, the members had all appeared very happy. She met people whose lives had been turned around since joining the group. They had found a place where they could truly be themselves and find inner joy and peace.

The group provided Maggie with financial independence from her parents and convinced her that this would allow her to reconnect with her daughter. Now, Maggie knew the chances of this happening were slim, but even a remote possibility had her hooked. Nevertheless, she had just swapped dependence on her parents for reliance on the group. She had no means of earning money to save. She merely worked for her keep, doing laundry, cleaning, and knitting small garments like hats and baby booties. The group sold the knitted items, produce from the land, and cheese made from their goats' milk at a local market. Some of the group members were musicians who played at the same market.

Jess was intrigued as she continued reading while lying on her bed, with her enormous belly and swollen ankles. She only had a few more weeks left at work before she began her maternity leave, and she wasn't going to miss being on her feet all day.

Jess really hoped that Maggie had found true happiness, but as she read on, she feared that Maggie's well-meaning, self-sufficient group may well be some sort of cult or at least highly manipulative, by how the leaders approached their role.

She could see how the group had managed to manipulate Maggie and used psychological techniques to prey on her vulnerable state. Instead of telling her what she wanted, they got her to articulate it, making her feel that the idea was her own. They were trying to give her a sense of freedom in her decision-making while actually controlling her for their own benefit. In the future, Maggie would be less likely to disagree with the group because, in effect, she'd be disagreeing with herself.

Once you say what you feel out loud, which Maggie did when she first met Susan, that becomes a part of your identity. Unfortunately, by doing so, you've taken the first big step to identifying with the cult. Initially, the group gave Maggie what she wanted – financial independence from her parents, whom she blamed for giving up Nancy. They also gave her a safe place where she could talk openly about her experiences of pregnancy, birth and those early days of holding Nancy and being a mother.

Jess completely understood why Maggie had decided to join the community. She'd even silently encouraged Maggie at times as she turned the pages of her diary. But now Jess was unsure. Was this the right place for her? Could she really find true friendship or joy here? She had closed off from her previous existence, so wasn't she still in a position where she was denying parts of herself? The 'cult' didn't even need to work on isolating her from her family and friends. Maggie did that herself. She hadn't even told Alice where she was going for fear that her parents would prise the information out of her. With each passing day, Maggie became increasingly dependent on the group.

22 March 1961

Today, I went with Susan and Bee to sell our products at the Grassington market. It's the first time I've been, and I was excited to get out of the community since I haven't been out anywhere since I got here. Susan left Bee and me to run the stall for a while as she had seen a young woman who was upset, so she was going to take her for a cup of tea and see if she was okay. At the market, I met Derrick. He's tall, handsome and quite charming. We exchanged polite conversation for some time. As he left, he winked at me and asked if I'd be at the stall again next week.

2 April 1961

I have recently started volunteering at the market stall each week to see Derrick. He works on his dad's dairy farm and has two younger sisters. He names his cows alphabetically and asked me for suggestions for the next calf to be born, which had to begin with 'J'. I suggested Joan or Jack, but Derrick preferred Jolie or Joyce. I asked Susan if Derrick could visit the community. She suggested he join us for a gathering. I said I'd ask him. Many communes, like Bright Light Living, offered non-resident member options for those who wanted to financially support the group without living there. In exchange, they could participate in group meals and meditation sessions. Derrick was to be asked if this was something might be interested in.

7 April 1961

I've invited Derrick to a community group. We'll be having a meal, and he's going to bring milk and eggs from his farm. Hopefully, we can sit next to each other, but usually, the group uses a small drawstring bag with everyone's name in. The names are drawn at random and placed on the table. The idea is that we will all have something to offer each other: a life story, a new perspective on a problem or sometimes a practical tip like how to grow the tallest sunflower or how to knit a blanket.

Some communes bar members from dating to avoid interpersonal conflict that could affect the stability, status or wider reputation of the group.

16 April 1961

Derrick and I were seated close to each other, close enough to hear each other's conversations and smile and nod to each other. We were at opposite sides of the long table, but it was still nice to hear him telling his farming stories to those next to him. I just can't believe what happened after the meal, though. I had offered to walk Derrick out so we could talk on the way, just the two of us.
We held hands once we were out of sight of the others, and I thanked him for coming. It had been so nice to show him where I lived.
He told me he had a lovely evening, and everyone had been very welcoming. He said the food and the company, especially mine, had been great.
I blushed as I told him I enjoyed his company too. We moved closer together, gazing into each other's eyes, and I thought he might kiss me until Susan suddenly appeared.
"Maggie," she shouted my name sternly, "you must say goodnight to our guest now." She then more or less asked Derrick to leave, but more politely than she'd just spoken to me. She thanked

him for joining us but stared at us impatiently. Derrick politely nodded to Susan, kissed my hand and wished me goodnight. Just as Derrick left, Susan grabbed hold of my arm. "How dare you," she shouted. "How dare you make such a fool of me, taking advantage of our community."

I was so shocked that I couldn't speak. I didn't say anything. Susan dragged me to our home and into my room, pushing me inside the doorway so hard that I stumbled backwards, falling to the floor. When I heard the door lock, I quickly jumped to my feet. It was locked. The doors had never been locked before. I don't have a key, and I certainly had not known that Susan had one. I sat on the floor in disbelief, with so many thoughts and emotions running through my mind. What have I done wrong? Had I been foolish to come here? Maybe I wasn't supposed to bring friends here to the community, but I had asked first and was told it was okay. Did Susan not like Derrick? Why was she so angry? Even Mum and Dad have never grabbed me in such a way in all those heated arguments before I left. It wasn't right. I've been totally blindsided. I'm tired now. I'm going to bed. I'll try to sleep, but my arm is still hurting, and Susan's words are still ringing in my ears.

It was now becoming clear that Maggie's participation in the group was in exchange for her freedom.

Chapter Four

Jess was home with this baby – her baby. She was a mother. Something she thought she'd never be. She did love the baby, at least she thought she did, but she had not experienced a rush of love at the birth. And while she'd been quite well during the pregnancy, the birth had been traumatic and had taken away any chance of this magical mother and baby bond she was always hearing about. She had an emergency caesarean section after 15 hours of labour, and the baby was becoming distressed. She was alone for the labour and birth, apart from the midwives.

She certainly wasn't in love with the fact that she had not slept for more than three hours in the last four days. She was struggling to get any sleep, even with the help of the nurses on the ward. One of the nurses had suggested she try morphine. Jess refused it initially, but the nurse said all the other women who had had the same procedure today had taken it and that she highly recommended Jess did too. She said it would help her sleep, but it left her tired and wired, her brain spinning with so many thoughts.

Later, around 1 am, a male nurse checked on her and the baby. He gently asked, "Why aren't you sleeping?"

"I can't," Jess replied. "I've tried."

"Well, let me know if you need anything."

At 2 am, Jess buzzed the nurse. "The baby's been sick, and I can't reach her." Jess was still recovering from the surgery and had a catheter bag attached to the side of the bed.

"I can do that," he said. "Where are your spare clothes for the baby?"

Jess pointed to the pile of tiny clothes on the chair.

"Do you have a name for her yet?" he asked as he carefully changed the baby.

Jess shook her head. "Not yet."

Now, back at home, she needed to settle on a name. But she wanted to get it right. She thought about naming the baby after her mum, Elizabeth. It was definitely an option. Jess's mum had died when she was just ten months old, so she had no memory of her. Her dad had shown her photographs, so she had always been able to imagine her. But as much as she liked the name, it made her feel sad when she thought of it, so it might not be fair to the baby. She didn't know how her mother had died as she was too young to remember, and as she grew, if she asked Dad, it just made him sad, so she stopped asking. She only knew that she had become ill after giving birth to her. Maybe Elizabeth could be her middle name? Elizabeth is of Hebrew origin, meaning "God's promise" or "God's oath".

Jess loved her stepmother, Jasmine. She and Jess's dad had married when Jess was seven years old. Jess had been a flower girl and had worn a beautiful white dress that matched Jasmine's bridal gown. Jasmine had always made Jess feel special, and with no children of her own, she had focused all her love and attention on her stepdaughter. Jasmine was always happy and smiling. Jess sometimes felt guilty for having such a good relationship with Jasmine, like she was betraying her mother somehow.

The name Jasmine is of Persian origin, meaning "gift from God". It is derived from the Persian word "Yasmin", referring to the plant meaning "fragrant flower".

"Yes," thought Jess, "that's the name. Yasmin." She had decided. Yasmin Elizabeth.

In the first few days after Yasmin was born, Jess had trouble getting her to latch for feeding. The nurses had been there to help her, but now they were home, the problem seemed to be worsening. The pain from breastfeeding had gradually increased for Jess, and Yasmin was losing more and more weight. The community midwife had suggested alternating between formula milk and breastfeeding to avoid the need for being readmitted to hospital.

Yasmin was constantly crying and distressed. It was obvious she was frustrated and hungry. Jess was determined she could do this alone, so she persevered. She would feel like she'd failed if she introduced formula milk.

It was 4 am. Jess and Yasmin had had no sleep. Jess thought about how sleep deprivation was used in torture, and she could now fully understand why.

Lack of sleep can lead to poor cognitive function, increased inflammation, and reduced immune function. If sleep deprivation continues, it may increase your risk for chronic disease.

Twenty-four-hour sleep deprivation is the same as having a blood alcohol concentration of 0.10 per cent. That's higher than the legal driving limit. When you miss 36 hours of sleep, your symptoms become more intense, and you'll have an overwhelming urge to sleep.

You may start experiencing microsleeps or brief periods of sleep without realizing it. A microsleep usually lasts up to 30 seconds, and during these periods, different parts of your brain will have difficulty communicating with each other. This severely impairs your cognitive performance. Missing sleep for 48 hours is known as extreme sleep deprivation and can cause hallucinations, where you might see, hear, or feel things that aren't actually there. People can experience depersonalization, anxiety, heightened stress levels and depression during this stage.

After three days of sleep loss, your urge to sleep will worsen, and you may experience more frequent, longer microsleeps. Sleep deprivation will significantly impair your perception, and

your hallucinations might become more complex. You may also have delusions and disordered thinking.
After four days, your perception of reality will be severely distorted, and your urge for sleep will feel unbearable. If you miss so much sleep that you're unable to interpret reality, this is called sleep deprivation psychosis.

Jess was still not allowed to drive, but there was a 24-hour garage a short walk away that she knew sold baby formula. She got up and dressed in yesterday's clothes she had taken off before bed which were still lying on the floor. She wrapped a screaming Yasmin up warmly in her pram and made her way to the garage. She returned home with the ready-made newborn formula, complete with teat, as she didn't have bottles or sterilisation equipment as she had planned to breastfeed exclusively. She offered the formula to Yasmin, who was obviously starving. She sucked so fast that the formula was gone in a minute. Finally, Yasmin was soothed for the first time and fell fast asleep, as did Jess. They both slept through four whole hours.

The next morning, Jess decided to stop breastfeeding. Her nipples were bleeding and sore, and Yasmin was a hungry baby who was content with the formula milk. Bothe of them had enjoyed a sound sleep.

But when you stop breastfeeding, your estrogen and progesterone levels start to fluctuate again. For some women who are sensitive to those changes, weaning can lead to mood swings. Additionally, the levels of oxytocin (that feel-good hormone) and prolactin decrease as estrogen and progesterone levels rise.

Jess stared down the dark hole of existence. She was sleep-deprived and overwhelmed from parenting alone. Her hormones returned to restart her menstrual cycle. She'd go off to sleep well enough after putting Yasmin down about midnight, but within the hour or so, she would wake with a start. Anxious thoughts would race through her mind. She'd ask herself if these intrusive thoughts were a sign of mental illness or if they were logical and understandable.
After checking Yasmin's breathing, Jess tried to steady her anxious mind. But the harder she tried the more the intrusive thoughts brought panic to her entire body. She knew she needed to be asleep while Yasmin was asleep before she woke for her next feed. This, and the pressure to sleep, made everything worse. She was so frustrated.
Every living thing dies. Everyone dies. This thought perpetrated her mind. Forget it, think of something else. She shook her head to shoo away the thought, but it didn't work.
It's a countdown, you see, from the moment a life begins. From when your baby is born. How will I explain that to her? I brought her here to die. I can't protect her from that.

You're just tired, she told herself. Remember, sleep deprivation can cause delusions, depression, anxious thoughts. Just breathe, Jess, just breathe. She tried to calm herself. The thoughts continued. *Even if it's an old person who falls into a deathly sleep, warm in their bed after decades of a well-lived life, by its very nature, a full, joyous life will leave someone behind. Grown children will still cry, Mummy, Daddy, I miss you. Where are you? Where did you go? Where did they go? Alive one minute. Dead the next.*
Shh, please stop. I need to sleep. Yasmin will want another feed soon. If I could just sleep. She lay her head on her pillow.
Do they leave their lifeless body, which remains but without their life force, will decay? Is it just over, gone?
Stop, please, stop. Yasmin is here, she is safe. I'm safe. I will sleep eventually. It will be OK.

Over the next few weeks, Jess's health deteriorated. She tried to push through after having consulted the midwives, who talked to her about the baby blues and how it was quite normal to feel low at times.
Jess could drive again as she had recovered from the surgery, so she decided to go for a drive with Yasmin to get out of the house. The motion soothed Yasmin, and she fell asleep. Jess took some deep breaths, trying to enjoy the silence. She couldn't. Her head was full of noise – a rush of intrusive thoughts. As she stopped the car at a level crossing, the barrier descended, and the lights flashed to allow a train to go. Suddenly, the thoughts stopped. The train whizzed past, and as

the road barrier opened again, the racing thoughts were replaced with just one calm voice saying, "I can understand it. I can. Why someone would go lay on the train track and wait for a train to come. Why it might be an option to find an escape from life, from yourself, from your thoughts, from the same struggle day after day."

The car behind Jess beeped. She looked at Yasmin in the rear-view mirror, put the car in gear and continued driving.

When Jess arrived home, Yasmin was still sleeping. Rather than risk waking her by carrying her into the house, Jess decided to wait in the car. As she sat there, she felt an odd sense of detachment from reality, like a strange stillness masquerading as peace. The thought in her mind was suggesting at least there was an option if things didn't improve. If things don't get a little bit easier, the option is there – to give up. She clenched her teeth so tightly that her whole mouth was aching, and her gums were bleeding. She tried to release the tension, but she was fuelled by tension and stress. It was running her entire system. If she let go of it, she might collapse in a heap, unable to form her structure to continue, like a used balloon that had released all its air. Unfillable, no form, no shape, no bounce. She was surviving every minute, existing in a void, spiralling endlessly in a great chasm between reality and complete detachment from it.

The next day, Jess rang her GP surgery. She waited on hold, listening to the pre-recorded message. "There are no more appointments available today. Please hang up and call back tomorrow unless it's urgent." She hung up, shaking, her heart pounding. It had taken her an hour to pick up her mobile, eventually scrolling to the doctor's number. She hesitated and then finally dialled, realizing it was now or never. She dialled again, this time waiting in the queue. Eventually, a lady answered. "Name?"

"… erm, it's… Jess Briar." Her voice was shaking. "Date of birth?"

Jess went blank for a moment as anxiety flooded her body. Then she remembered.

"July. 1st of July 1989."

"And what's the problem?"

Jess wasn't sure how to answer, but she tried. "Erm, yes, well. Since my baby girl was born, I've been, erm, struggling."

She waited for a response from the lady on the other end of the phone, but there wasn't one. She took it from the silence that she needed to give more information to hit the threshold required to speak with a doctor. So she tried to be more specific, feeling very uncomfortable doing so.

"I've not been sleeping, and I've been feeling down and quite anxious, and I feel I need to speak to a doctor."

"We only have emergency appointments left. Do you feel like it's an emergency?"

"Erm. Well, I suppose, erm, not really."

"In that case, I'll take some notes, and the doctor will ring you at some point, but it won't be today."

"Okay. Thanks," said Jess

"Bye." Said the lady and hung up the phone.

Jess placed her mobile on the side table and started to cry. Yasmin woke up and began to cry. Jess picked her up and held her, and they cried together.

Later that week, Jess spoke to a doctor, who scheduled a face-to-face appointment with her. Of course, she would have to take Yasmin with her as she didn't have anyone she trusted to look after her. Fortunately, Yasmin was asleep. She had to carry Yasmin in her arms as pushchairs were not allowed in the surgery. She had lifted her ever so gently, praying to anyone who would listen that she wouldn't wake.

Jess sat in the waiting area for what felt like an eternity. She could hear the large clock on the wall ticking, mocking her, the seconds passing excruciatingly slowly. Jess practised what she was going to say. She felt like running away. Finally, her name was called, and her whole body jerked like someone had just fired a weapon in her direction.

She entered the doctor's room, feeling fragile. The name on the door said Dr T Addie.

"Hello. What can I do for you today, Mrs Briar?" Dr Addie asked, half-smiling when she saw Yasmin in Jess's arms.

"It's Miss, actually," Jess said.

"Miss Briar. My apologies."

Jess paused, and then the words flew out of her in a jumble she hoped the doctor would understand. "Since I had my daughter, it's just been, well, it's been hard. I've not been sleeping, and, well, I don't have family nearby, and my emotions have been up and down. Well, more down, actually. I guess if I'm being honest, when Yasmin is sleeping, and I should be asleep, I start to get anxious thoughts. Then I get more tired and more overwhelmed, and it becomes a vicious circle. I can cope with being a single mother. I'll always put her first, don't worry about that. I'm not saying I can't do it. Well, I have to do it, but I feel like I might need some sort of help." She didn't stop to take a breath until she had finished.

"Hmm," Dr Addie responded, glancing up at Jess from her computer screen, "I see." She glanced back down as though reading from a script on the screen.

"Have you ever felt like this before?"

"Before?" Jess repeated the question to herself, thinking about it. "Not like this. I've had dips into low moods, but I've always managed it. Same with anxiety, I've always managed it myself."

"So, just since you gave birth?"

Jess nodded in agreement.

"I could prescribe you a medication. Just a low dose to take in the short term. It will help with the anxiety and low mood." She tapped the keys on her computer and then reached into her drawer, producing a leaflet. If you feel you need to, there's a telephone number you can ring on here to refer yourself for some CBT therapy. There is a 9-month waiting list, however." She paused for half a second, looked up at Jess, and said, "Is there anything else?"

"Erm, no," said Jess, flustered. "Thanks."

Jess stood back out in the corridor and glanced up at the clock. Five minutes she had been in there. If only that was all it would take – a five-minute consultation and some magic pills. Still, that was all she had, so hopefully, the medication would help her.

The medication did help Jess. She still was extremely anxious, but she found it easier to cope. Although the anxious thoughts were still intrusive, her logical mind was more agile and able to navigate them logically before deepening into a panic attack. She knew she was still in desperate need of some solid sleep, and she knew it was time to ask her dad for help.
He and Jasmin were currently in Luxembourg, but they spoke every other day around lunchtime, and today was his day to call. There was only a one-hour time difference.
Jess had taken Yasmin for a walk in the pushchair to get her to nap. The pushchair was now back in the hallway with a sleeping Yasmin. Jess had tiptoed into the kitchen, made herself a cup of tea, and now sat on the sofa with her phone in her hand, ring volume turned down, waiting for her dad to call. She didn't have long to wait. Her phone flashed and vibrated quietly. 'Dad!'
"Hello, love, how are you? We're just having a spot of lunch, sitting outside a bistro with beautiful views. Jas says hello and asks how little Yasmin is doing. She is still so chuffed you named her after her," said Ian.
"That's lovely, Dad. Is the sun out?"

"Aye, it's a beautiful day again," he responded.
"Dad?" said Jess.
"Yes, love," he said.
"Do you think you could come home now for a bit? Meet Yasmin? I know I said not to rush, but it feels like the right time. I need my family."
"Of course, darling, I told you I would come home if you needed me. And we can't wait to meet our granddaughter."
Jess started to cry. She tried to muffle her sobs, but she couldn't.
"Are you okay, love?"
"I'm a bit emotional, Dad, and so happy I'll be seeing you soon."
"Well, listen, we could be home in a few days. We're not so far from Calais. I'll look at the ferries this afternoon and update you. Is she asleep now, the little one?"
"Yes, Dad."
"And have you got yourself a cup of tea?"
"Yes, Dad."
"Good, good. Be seeing you soon, love."
"Yes. Great. Thanks, Dad. Safe journey. Keep in touch."
"I will, love."
"Bye, Daddy."
"Bye."

****

Jess's dad and stepmother had been staying with her for a week already. They had decorated the spare room so they could stay there and took Yasmin in with them every other night. They had prepared Jess beautiful, nutritious meals and entertained Yasmin so Jess could tend to everyday things like taking a shower. They had both provided Jess with so much love and practical support, as well as listening to her and providing emotional support as far as they could.

One day, while Yasmin was sleeping the sun came out, so Ian suggested that he and Jess take a walk together. Although Jess didn't like to be away from Yasmin, even in the house, Ian wanted to talk to her, and they wouldn't go far.

"Jasmine will be here if she wakes. We'll stay close by," reassured Ian.

Jess reluctantly agreed.

The breeze felt nice on her face as they strolled along the path next to a farm.

"Dad?" Jess asked out of the blue." What happened to mum?"

"I wanted to speak to you about that, Jess. I should have done so before now, and I'm sorry I haven't, darling."

Jess gave him a look, which suggested he should continue.

"Your mother also struggled with her mental health after you were born. She'd always been a worrier, and it became worse after your birth. She was always on edge and would get angry over small things. She was living on her nerves. But she loved you very much. I once found her just gazing at you, saying, "My darling girl, you are so beautiful. You are such a gift. You bring me moments of pure joy. I just wish I was here." I asked her what she meant by this. As I could only see things through a logical lens, she was clearly here – with me and baby you.

She then said she felt like a piece of her mind had been taken. She was aware of her surroundings and what was happening, but she was watching through a murky, dark glass. No matter how hard she tried, she couldn't break through it because the piece of her mind that knew how to was gone. Just like getting stuck in quicksand, the harder she struggled, the more she became stuck living there behind the murky, dark-tinted, thick glass that took away all of life's colours, the ability to be present and the joy of being a mother in all its glory. Yet she still had to function, especially in that role as a mother. You understand that now.

Jess nodded, tears filling her eyes as they sat on the dry stone wall. The weight of her father's words was crushing her, and she needed to stop for a minute and rest whilst she took it all in. It took all her energy.

"I didn't really get it at first, I'm ashamed to say," her father continued. "She looked to be coping fine. She would repeatedly say she was tired, but I thought that was normal with a new baby. I was tired too. But her tiredness was different, and she didn't know how to express it. She was tired before the day began. She was trying so hard to be how she was before, and that was exhausting. Impossible. On top of this, her monthlies returned. You know."

"Yes, Dad. Her periods."

"Well, yes. And heavy, much heavier than before she had you. I took her to the doctor when I realised it was more than just ordinary tiredness. They did various tests, blood pressure that kind of thing. Felt her stomach. Asked if she was eating and sleeping well. They couldn't find anything physically wrong.

Well, I think this made her more depressed – you know, that the doctors couldn't help. Couldn't 'fix' her. There were moments she'd return to us. Happy and laughing. Had the energy to play. Take you to the park, but they were all too fleeting." He reached over and held Jess's hand. "My darling daughter, I've never known how or when to tell you this, but she lost the fight. She ran out of reserves eventually. Not even you or I could pull her through anymore. She became so mentally unwell she couldn't see a way forward." Jess's father sighed and touched his forehead, rubbing gently as if the words needed help leaving his head. He continued, "When she passed, it was suicide."

He took Jess's hands into his own, and tears rolled down both their cheeks. His voice cracked as he spoke: "It just can't happen again. I won't let it happen to you or to Yasmin."

Jess fell into his arms, sobbing from the pit of her stomach. Deep, mournful cries. Her dad held her and whispered, "I'm here for as long as you need me, my darling." Then, after a few minutes of silence, he added, "Your mother's doctors were wrong."

Jess sat up and wiped her eyes. "What do you mean?"

"There was a reason she was ill. If I'd have known, then what I know now."

"What do you know now, Dad?"

"As soon as I found out you were pregnant, I began researching, googling symptoms, finding research papers, I've even joined social media groups. I was scared that giving birth might affect you in the same way. I believe your mother and, unfortunately, dear, yourself have PMDD. Premenstrual Dysphoric Disorder. I'm going to help you get a diagnosis and proper treatment."

"What?"

"Something changed in your mum. It wasn't just tiredness or heavy periods, but there was no help. After decades of thinking about the hows and whys, I needed to know you'd be safe. That Yasmin would have a mother. That I'd still have my daughter."

"Is it postnatal depression, Dad? Why is there a monster in my head? It has a voice like mine, but it's not me. It makes me grind my teeth. It makes me hold tension in my head. It makes my arms and legs feel like lead. It bullies me and tells me bad things will happen. It tells me things will never get better, just worse. It makes my eyes so heavy and sleepy, but my mind and my heart are going so fast I can't rest. My ears ring. I feel sick but also so hungry that I crave food constantly. My face swells, my tummy swells, my skin feels uncomfortable, like I want to crawl out of my own body to escape. I feel light-headed."

"I think it's triggered by the birth, but I don't believe it's postnatal depression. Not with your symptoms and your mother's history and that you're not feeling better with medication. I believe it could be Premenstrual Dysphoric Disorder. Let's go home, and I can tell you more after we've had a cuppa."

Jess sobbed again. This time, it felt like a release. Father and daughter held hands as they walked back to 33 Upper Float Road. "I won't leave you," Ian said. "Jas and I are both here for you and Yasmin."

Chapter Five

"I'm here," Ian whispered, squeezing Jess's hand as they waited in the doctor's surgery. When Jess had noticed it was Dr Addie again, she nearly bolted for the door. The big clock was mocking her again, every tick reverberating throughout her body. Small movements that the untrained eye probably could not see took over her body. She was slightly rocking forward as if all her muscles were switching to stand and flee, but then they would relax again like she was superglued to the chair. Her breath became shallow, and she felt sick and slightly dizzy. Her teeth were biting together, and her heart beat out of rhythm.

Finally, her name was called. Jess stood up. Ian did too. She didn't look at him because she was trying not to cry. She knew he was there, and that was enough as she feared she would revert to a little girl and throw herself into his arms, crying, "Take me home, Daddy."

As she walked towards the doctor's door, she could barely control her wobbly legs. She sat on the chair nearest to Dr Addie, and Ian sat beside her.

"Hello again, Jess. How are you? And who do you have with you today?" said Dr Addie, turning away from the computer to face Jess and her father.

Jess was taken aback, as just a few weeks ago, she had hardly looked up from her computer screen. She was relieved that the doctor had at least remembered her.

"I'm Ian, Jess's father."

"It's nice to meet you. Jess, how have you found the tablets?"

"Erm, well, erm…" Jess fiddled with her hands and said, "They've helped a little, I suppose, and having Dad home is great, but I'm still unwell."

"Yes, it can take time for the tablets to work. Will you keep on with them?"

"I will," replied Jess, feeling defeated.

"Doctor," said Jess's dad with confidence.

Dr Addie looked at him. "My wife took her own life when Jess was just ten months old. The fact that this is now happening to Jess and for me to see her so physically and mentally unwell is devastating for us as a family. But that was over 30 years ago, so I've reassured Jess that she won't be left to face this without proper medical support from you. Am I right?"

Dr Addie nodded, and Ian continued.

"Jess has all the symptoms of PMDD. Now, Dr Addie, could you use your computer to open the NICE guidance please. Thank you." He dug into his coat pocket and produced some papers. "I took the liberty of printing out the treatment options from the International Association of Premenstrual Disorders."

Dr Addie appeared flustered but remained professional. She quickly skimmed through the papers Ian had produced and referenced the NICE guidance. After a few minutes, she spoke, "Yes, alright. SSRIs are the medication I prescribed for you. Let's increase your dose and see if that helps. Keep a diary of your symptoms to determine if it could be PMDD, and come back in, let's say, three months."

17 April 1961

This morning, Susan, Mike and Thomas came to my room, which they must have unlocked while I was sleeping. They knocked politely, and Susan said sweetly, "Can we come in?" Before I had a chance to answer, the three of them entered. "We'd like you to come with us to eat breakfast." Still shell-shocked, I agreed. We didn't go to the community space as usual; instead, they took me to a small canteen adjacent to the offices, a place I'd never been before. I guess they chose here for privacy. We all sat down, and Susan poured me a cup of tea. Thomas spoke first. He gently asked how I was feeling about being away from Nancy. Then Mike told me how they valued me as a member of the community and that, in future, he would suggest I focus on my 'why' – why I'd come to the community. Then, Susan opened the top drawer of the side table, and there it was – a photograph of my baby girl. I can't believe it. It's like holding her in my arms again. I can look at her every day. It's not the best quality photograph, quite blurred, but it's mine to cherish.

Jess was mentally screaming down through the diary pages to Maggie, "Run, escape, don't stay there, it's all lies. That's not a picture of your Nancy, it's a generic, blurred picture presented to a mother so desperate that she'll believe it and not see the reality of the situation. Don't stay there, Maggie. Don't fall for it!"

Jess felt like all her nerve endings were on the outside of her body, raw and exposed. She had real empathy for Maggie, two mothers trying to negotiate two difficult situations. They both needed help to navigate their way out of the dark places where they had found themselves.

Jess felt like she had been drugged and was emotionally vulnerable. Her eyes were glazed over, and her body ached from top to toe, battered by waves of nausea. She felt sick if she ate, and she felt sick if she didn't. Her body craved food, but she fluctuated from being ravenous to feeling sick, her face drawn and pale like she was aboard a ship in turbulent seas. She felt physically and emotionally overwhelmed. If one more tiny event was placed on her load, she might descend into utter despair.

She was so bloated around her stomach that all her clothes felt comfortable. She was retaining so much water that her face felt fat, and her rings wouldn't fit. Her face was covered in spots, and she couldn't wear jewellery as it irritated her skin. When she showered and washed her hair, it felt exhausting, as if she'd run a marathon.

She felt like there was a barrier between herself and the real world. Although she felt different inside, on the outside, she appeared normal, and nobody seemed to be able to see how much she was suffering, how much she was struggling. It hurt to stand up, but it was tiring j just to sit. She relied on caffeine and chocolate to provide small pockets of energy to function as a mother. She couldn't tolerate changes in temperature. She was usually quick to feel the cold, but now hot flushes, rashes and swellings would come in waves, making her light-headed. She'd remove layers to cool down, and shortly after, she'd be shivering. Noises startled her, sending her heart to beat wildly.

Jess was two months into the three-month period when the doctor had asked her to keep a diary. It was clear now that her symptoms were linked to her menstrual cycle. She had learnt the names for the different cycle phases, and this hellish time of ramped-up symptoms she now knew was called the luteal phase – the time between ovulation and the start of her monthly bleed. For Jess, this was two weeks out of every four. She would then bleed heavily for seven days, enduring severe cramps and extreme fatigue. Following this, she would have one 'normal' week in the follicular phase after her period, before ovulation and the return of the luteal phase and its torrential downpour of life-limiting symptoms.

Jess despaired that she would have to wait another month before getting help. She understood the theory of keeping the diary to track the numerous symptoms to get the precise diagnosis, but three months of feeling so mentally and physically unwell is a long time.

She went downstairs. Jasmine and Ian were playing on the floor with Yasmin. They had her stacking bricks, encouraging her to build and then applauding, signalling her to knock them down again. Yasmin clapped along too.

"The kettle's just boiled, love. Do you want a brew?" Ian said.

"Okay, thanks, Dad. I'll do it. You stay and play with Yasmin." Jess managed a smile and walked into the kitchen. Dad had already set out a mug with a teabag in it. She poured the water and went to the fridge to get the milk. Somehow, between the fridge and the worktop, Jess managed to trip over her own feet and splash milk everywhere as the lid wasn't on properly. "Stupid milk," she muttered. Dad appeared at the door.

"Here," he said, picking up a cloth. Jess took the cloth and Dad finished making her tea, taking out the teabag before it got too strong while she wiped the milk from the floor. Jess would be so clumsy during the luteal phase. It was like her body and mind weren't her own, and there was a delay in their communication with each other. Even her thought process was taken over. Usually a reasonable, level-headed person, Jess would be thwarted by black-and-white thinking. Everything was either wonderful or awful, and either option would leave her in tears. If someone let her go ahead of them in a supermarket queue or smiled and said good morning on her walk with Yasmin, she would be overcome with emotion, over-appreciating their kindness. Equally, if someone took her parking space or forgot to say thank you, she was like the manners police. She would become agitated and couldn't always hold her tongue. She would be rude back, and this was so out of character for Jess that the whole experience of just popping to the shops would overwhelm her.

Ian and Jasmine had cancelled their immediate travel plans as nothing was more important to them than making sure Jess and Yasmin were okay and that there was no chance of history repeating itself.

1 May 1961

I haven't seen Derrick again as I couldn't go to the market. When I asked, Susan didn't
 say no directly; she just said it was someone else's turn, but I heard the no. I suppose she thinks it's what's best for me. I dreamt about Nancy last night. She'll be eight months old now. I wonder how she's growing and changing. Would we even know each other if we saw each other ever again. Would we look like each other? I pray that her adoptive parents love her as much as I do. I

couldn't bear it if her life wasn't filled with joy and happiness. The thought that she would have a better life than the one I could give her gets me through each waking minute. The only glimpse of happiness I felt in the past year was my time in Derrick's company, and now that's over too.

One morning, Jess told her dad about the diary she had found. It was a good distraction from her own thoughts and took them to a world outside of this strange holding pattern they'd found themselves in. Ian had said that Maggie's situation seemed like coercion and that the group she had joined sounded very much like a cult. He explained that cults are predatory, and they had preyed on Maggie because she was vulnerable.

"Apex predators are omnivores," Ian said. "They have options, so if they think you'll be easily overcome, that's it for you, but if they think you'll put up a fight, they'll likely opt for smaller prey."

"I never imagined when I bought this house, Maggie's home, that I'd uncover such detail about her or that it would have been filled with such sadness," said Jess.

"I'd never really thought about adoption from a young mother's point of view, I'm ashamed to say." Ian continued, "After I met your mother's parents for the first time, she told me on the way home that she was adopted. Her parents told her they had always wanted a child and were blessed by having her in their life. She said she'd grown up happy, and we never really talked about it again. She presumed that her biological mother had believed she was giving her a better life and never questioned it further. I guess there's always a winner and a loser."

"It's awful how her parents shut her down. Imagine having to deny such a massive part of yourself. For them to insist it was a discretion and one that should never be mentioned again. If they had supported her better and shown her love, she wouldn't have been preyed on by this group," said Jess.

"I now wonder what your mum's birth mother's circumstances were. Who she was. At the time, I just knew your mother was happy and had a good relationship with your grandparents, and that's all I needed to know and all she needed too, it seemed," said Ian.

"Do you think we could try and find out, Dad? Do you think we should?" asked Jess.

"She may not still be alive, but yes, let's do it… for all of us."

"All of us?" Jess said, confused.

"Yes, all the women. Yasmin, you, Elizabeth and her mother, your grandmother. Let's put the pieces together. It feels fitting right now."

"And are you sure you're okay to stay, Dad? You and Jasmine are giving up your retirement adventure."

"My dear, we're not giving it up, we're just pressing pause for a while. And, anyway, having you has always been my biggest adventure."

When Jess found out she was pregnant, she contacted Benjamin. He was evasive at first, not responding to her calls or messages, but he eventually picked up the phone. She'd wanted to see him face-to-face to tell him the news, but he had refused a meeting, saying that it was better if they didn't see each other again, so she'd had to blurt it out right there and then on the phone. After a minute's silence, Benjamin had hung up. Jess didn't attempt to call him straight back. She left him to digest the information. It had been a shock to her, too, on first finding out.

Benjamin had rung back a few days later. At the time, it was like he had swallowed a self-help book. He was very measured in his comments and spoke to her softly, "I will be there for our baby. Even though we aren't together anymore, we can be mature and make parenting work. Do you want me to come to the antenatal classes? I can do that and be there at the birth. Have you a due date yet? We can make a list of things we need to buy. Should we find out if it's a boy or a girl at the 20-week scan?" He'd obviously been doing his research. But that was the last time Jess heard from Benjamin. As the pregnancy progressed, she'd tried to call, but he never answered. She sent him messages with dates and times of scans, midwife appointments and antenatal classes, but he never responded. She used to watch the door at appointments just in case he decided to show up at the last minute. The last time she rang him was when she was in hospital about to be induced. She thought maybe he would want to be part of the birth so that he could meet his daughter. This time, when she called his number, she heard the message, "the number you have dialled has not been recognised. Please hang up and try again."

***

Jess and Ian had decided to start looking for information on Elizabeth's mother, Jesse's grandmother, the simplest way. The only information they had was her name, Peggy Lee. They sat side by side in Jesse's small home office and opened the Google search engine. Jess typed in Peggy's full name. Immediately, a list of various search results was loaded. It was hard to know what was relevant, if anything, and what wasn't. They began reading down the list.

Norma Deloris Egstrom [a] (May 26, 1920–January 21, 2002), known professionally as Peggy Lee, was an American jazz and popular music singer, songwriter, composer, and actress whose career spanned seven decades. Connect with PeggyLee29 on Instagram. Peggy Lee Obituaries.

"Well, I don't think your grandmother was Norma Deloris, so maybe social media and obituaries might be the place to start," said Ian. "However, we've no idea how old she'd be."

Jess suggested checking social media sites like Facebook, LinkedIn, Twitter, and Instagram. Ian was sure that the adoption was in Yorkshire but couldn't recall the exact location. He thought he might have the paperwork somewhere in storage. So, they searched Peggy Lee and filtered the results based on her likely location in Yorkshire. If they found anyone within the right age bracket and location, they could use the messaging feature to ask for more information. They knew this procedure wasn't going to be a quick or easy. Next, for a small fee, they took to the UK's electoral register as their next valuable resource. It lists the names of everyone registered to vote. They found a couple of Peggy Lees and noted the addresses and phone numbers so they could pick up the search again later in the week when, hopefully, they'd have some replies to their messages.

They also planned to join a genealogy website, Ancestry.co.uk or FindMyPast.co.uk, since these sites offered access to various historical records such as census data, birth, marriage and death certificates. Ian and Jasmine were going to visit Bradford Central Library, hoping to access local newspapers, historical events and other community records. Or perhaps the librarian could provide specific guidance on how and where to look for an adopted child's biological parents.

They had discussed hiring a private investigator, if necessary, but this was expensive, so they would exhaust all other options first.

25th November 1961

I feel so lonely here now. I Even although There are people around me, it feels like everything is on their terms. The "optional" activities are attended by everyone. Ray, a 'newbie', didn't show up at yesterday's morning share session, and, like me, I later saw him being ushered into the back-office kitchen. I miss my friends, Alice and Betty. I long to walk down to the stream, eating dolly mixtures, singing and dancing and splashing in the water. I long to tell Alice about everything that has happened this past year since I left home. I wonder how she is doing and what Betty and she have been up to. For the first time, I thought how worried everyone must have been when I just disappeared. When I just wanted to escape my life. I have decided I will write to Alice. I will have to plan it carefully, though, as contacting people outside the community is closely monitored. All mail sent directly from the community must have the leader's permission, and they read the contents. I'll have to find an opportunity to post it secretly. There is a postbox in town that I could reach on market day, so I need to be "good" – a model of compliance, so that I can be "trusted" to go to the market again.

It's not always obvious, but now I realise this community could be defined as a cult because of its control and isolation of individuals like myself from any connection to their past life or from making any new connection that might take you away from the group. While the group would not openly admit to being a cult, not being able to make my own choices and not being allowed to question anything or disagree with Susan or the other leaders would suggest they are.

Yet again, I am being controlled. Told what I can and cannot discuss, who I can and can't talk to or correspond with, even when out of the confinement of the community. This is why I left home in the first place. Because Mum and Dad were controlling my behaviour, not allowing me to acknowledge my pregnancy and making me lie to people about her very existence.

I can't believe a year has passed since I joined the group. Today, Nancy is one year, two months, one week and two days old. I can see now how easily the vulnerable can get pulled into a cult, but getting out of one is not so easy! If I'd have been wise, I would have had an exit strategy when I joined, just in case it didn't work out.

I am sticking to my plan to write to Alice in secret. There is no one I trust in here to confide in. If anyone suspected that I was trying to communicate with my friend from outside the community, they would monitor me closely, and then it would be impossible. I will participate in the meetings and activities as normal to avoid arousing any suspicion. I have already put my name on the market list rota. When I did so, Mabel, head of dishing out the monthly roles within the community, smiled and nodded. That is a good sign. Previously, she would say things like, "Your skills are best suited elsewhere this month" or " That role has been filled. Try again next month." In other words, we still don't trust you with strangers who might see through what we are actually doing here – people like Derrick. I have learned not to challenge the leaders as their suggestions are merely disguised orders. Fingers crossed, I will make the list for the coming month. I will write my letter to Alice in the hope that I can get out to the market and post it.

***

"There's limited research but what we do know is your brain reacts negatively to hormone fluctuations. And, as a woman, your hormones shift and change through your approximate 28-day cycle each month. The most stable time for your hormones in your cycle is the follicular phase, starting on the first day of your period and continuing up to the main event, ovulation. Ovulation itself and the hormone changes that follow is when hormones rise and fall, producing symptoms." The doctor continued, "The abnormal way that your brain reacts to these normal hormone fluctuations is what is causing your symptoms of depression, hopelessness, thoughts of self-harm or even suicide, irritability, tension and conflict with others. This also explains your anxiety, disinterest in your usual activities, sleep and concentration issues. Fatigue, forgetfulness, withdrawal, paranoia, and low self-confidence are other physical symptoms you've likely been suffering. Causing the changes in appetite, food cravings, cramps and bloating, joint pain, headaches, breast tenderness, hot flashes and bowel changes. People with PMDD have a neurobiological sensitivity to hormonal changes." After ten months, Jess was finally sitting in front of a doctor who was giving her answers. She had returned to her GP, Dr Addie, after three months with the information she had collected, showing a definitive connection between her menstrual cycle and her symptoms. Dr Addie wanted her to continue taking her anti-depression medication, drink herbal tea and find time for relaxation. Jess was already doing everything she possibly could to take care of her mental and physical health but had hit the ceiling because she had a condition that she could not regulate by herself. Luckily, her dad had been with her and requested a referral to see a gynaecologist as he felt Jess's symptoms were having a detrimental effect on her ability to live a normal life. The GP had agreed. And Jess had faced another wait until an appointment came through.

When the day of the appointment arrived, it didn't go well. Jess had left in floods of tears. The 'specialist' had never heard of PMDD. He said he could perform an endometrial ablation to remove a thin layer of tissue (endometrium) that lines the uterus to stop her heavy periods.

"At least you won't have heavy periods any more then just the other symptoms," he'd said dismissively. I preform several of these procedures every week. This was clearly his specialism, as could be seen by the many certificates on the wall. Or you can take the contraceptive pill. Jess was left with these two options: the procedure or to "take the pill". Not really understand how it would help, Jess agreed to take the pill.

When leaving the appointment, Ian said, "Well, he was a one-trick pony, wasn't he? You sneeze, and I can fix that with ablation surgery. Your finger is falling off, what you need is ablation surgery. I'm an expert, you know." At least he had managed to make Jess smile for a moment. She wasn't convinced that the doctors knew how to deal with her symptoms, but she would try anything to feel better.

Following this experience, Ian suggested finding a private consultant for an initial diagnosis – a consultant that might have at least heard of the condition. He offered to pay for it as Jess was not back at work.

And now here they were, in front of a doctor who understood what was happening to Jess. It was such a relief for them both. She would now have an official diagnosis of Premenstrual Dysphoric Disorder and could start on a pathway of treatments. It was a chronic illness that wasn't curable but was treatable once you'd found a medical professional who had heard of premenstrual Dysphoric Disorder.

Chapter Six

62 Years Before

"Alice, dear. You have a letter," called Jilly, Alice's mother.
"A letter? How exciting. I rarely get mail.
 I wonder who it's from," said Alice.
The letter read:

My dearest friend Alice,

I have missed you terribly this past year and hardly know where to begin my story. I hope you and your parents are well. How is Betty? I miss seeing you both all dressed up for an evening of dancing.

Have my parents been worried about me?
I am safe. I've been living in a community where everyone pitches in with the work and shares what they have.

I think I'm ready to leave and come home now, but it's not so easy once you've been part of a group like this for so long. Also, I'm not sure where I would go as my relationship with my parents is so fractured. At the minute, I only leave the community buildings to sell produce at Grassington market on a Saturday. I will try to sneak away from the stall this week for five minutes. The leaders here are not keen on us having contact with people outside, so I'll have to do it in secret and be careful not to be seen. I'll be on the corner of Acre Lane facing towards the market square. I'll wait under the large oak tree there, out of sight. Can you meet me? The market begins at 8 am. I'll get away when I can.

I can't give you a return address as we are not allowed to receive personal letters. And please don't tell anyone.

I'm sorry I left without saying goodbye. It's not an excuse, but I was so lost at that time and needed to escape. I knew if I'd told you, it would have been impossible for you to keep it from my parents, and I didn't want them to find me.

Please come.

Much love from your best friend,
Maggie xxx

The following Saturday, Alice got up early. She told her mother about the letter and swore her to secrecy, but her mother insisted on coming with her. They would take the bus from Ingleton to Grassington, which is about an hour's journey They had wrapped up warm as it was a cold December day with frost on the ground. Alice's mother had packed sandwiches and a flask of tea. When they boarded, the conductor collected their fare, and they settled in for the journey.
"So, has Maggie been here the whole time she's been missing?" Alice's mum asked.
"Yes, it seems that way from the letter. She didn't want her parents to find her, so she just left without saying a word."
"And she's meeting us in secret because the group won't allow her to have contact with us? Is that right?" Jilly was trying to figure out just what her role was today. And just what kind of situation Maggie had found herself in.
"Her letter said she'd have to be careful not to be seen talking to us and that she could only see me for five minutes," Alice confirmed.
"I understand why you don't want to tell her parents, but shouldn't we inform the police? She is a missing person," Jilly said with concern.
"I'm just doing what she asked. She's reached out to me, her best friend, and I want to reach back. I don't want to put her in danger or scare her off, or

we may never get her back. I don't know where the community is where she's been living, and I don't want her to disappear again." Alice began to question herself. Should she have called the police? But Maggie was a grown woman. If she had gone freely to this place and confirmed she wanted to be there, what could they do? They couldn't force her to come home.

Alice and her mother arrived at the bottom end of Acre Lane, facing the market square and found the oak tree mentioned in Maggie's letter. On the journey, they had agreed that Alice would meet her alone. So, Jilly found a bench a little further down the street to be nearby if needed. With Alice by the tree and her mother in position on the bench, they waited. Alice could see the market stalls in the square across the road.

The stalls were selling fresh eggs from the community chickens, roasted chestnuts, crocheted Christmas stockings and carved wooden nutcracker soldiers. The square was dressed in pretty, twinkling Christmas lights. In the far corner towards Acre Lane, the local church choir sang Christmas carols to raise money for the church roof repairs that were badly needed. The Community liked to be seen as supporting the local area's needs so as not to appear suspicious or worthy of gossip. In turn, they would send a group member, including Maggie, with some cash to join in the singing and make a donation. It was a show in itself, making them go over one at a time to ensure their involvement in the carol singing throughout the day. The singers always drew the biggest crowd. When it was Maggie's turn to go, she would slip unnoticed into the crowd.

Alice was determined she would stand in this exact spot all day if she had to, and she knew her mother would do the same, though her spot was a little more comfortable. Her mother, Jilly, ever prepared was wrapped up in several layers and her largest scarf. She had a little lap blanket and a thermos of tea. After an hour, Alice faced the possibility that Maggie may not show up. Her heart sank as she had no way to get in touch with her best friend. She couldn't bear the thought, so she let it slip away into the shadows of her mind. She did a little on-the-spot jog, clapped her hands together and wiggled her fingers to wake them up from the cold. She was here for the long haul.

Maggie watched Brendan take his turn to join the carol singers. She had hoped she would be asked to go first. She joined Susan at the stall. Maggie noticed how friendly and funny Susan was with the customers, charming even. She was so good at connecting with people, and everyone she spoke to made a purchase. It reminded her of the evening they had first met. Susan had made her feel seen, understood, safe. She'd thought they had a connection; otherwise, she would have never left with her. She could hardly believe the stark contrast between this woman and the Susan she now knew. Susan who ruled with an iron fist, who coerced and controlled a whole group of people. It was Maggie's turn to be charming and connect with Susan, so she could get what she wanted. She would become an actress, taking on the role of the conscientious, committed, unquestioning follower. Someone Susan could trust.

"Wow, Susan, I can't believe you have sold so many items. I am always trying to learn from your example. I know the income from this stall is essential to our community, and that's so important to me."

Susan looked pleased. "The trick is to make eye contact. That's how you first connect with a person. Smile and comment on how you like their scarf, their hat, their brooch. Make it about them, not the stall, and then they will want to reciprocate your kind gesture by making a purchase."

Maggie couldn't quite believe that Susan was sharing this information with her. It's precisely how she controls the community. But she smiled and nodded to show she was really interested, and Susan continued.

"If they mention who they are buying for – a daughter, a grandchild – you can use that. Ask about them and engage them by talking about someone they love. How can they then not buy them something? You see?"

Maggie nodded. "Oh, and the choir. The carol singers, everyone at the winter market loves to hear them. It's so great that you have always supported them. It cements our place here, doesn't it? People see that we are just normal, kind, compassionate people."

"Exactly. We have earned our place in the community. Every winter at the market, we sing with the choir and make a donation. It's become a tradition."

A tall lady with dark hair and green blue, wearing a beautiful navy woollen coat and matching leather gloves, approached the stall.

"May I say, madam, your leather gloves are exquisite. They go perfectly with your equally beautiful coat," said Susan with a sickly sweet smile that Maggie now saw as sinister.

"Thank you. My gloves are new. They were a gift. How nice of you to notice," said the lady.

"And the whole look – the navy brings out the colour of your stunning blue eyes," Susan continued to flatter.

"Thank you. Did you crochet these stockings?" enquired the lady.

"Yes, each and every one. They make such a thoughtful gift for someone special at this time of year. We use wool from a local farm," said Susan, now turning her praise onto the products as she snared her victim into her trap.

"I'm thinking of my grandson," said the lady.

That's it, thought Maggie. She's got you now that she knows who you're buying for.

"You have a grandson? How lovely. How old is he?" said Susan, tightening her grip on the poor, unsuspecting lady.

"Yes, he is eight," the lady answered.

"Oh, lovely. That is such a precious age," said Susan, smiling now and holding the lady's gaze.

"I would like to take a stocking, please, and half a dozen eggs," said the lady.

"Good choice," said Susan. "Which stocking would you like?"

Maggie brought over the eggs as the lady chose a stocking, and Susan took the payment.

When the lady had gone, Maggie turned to Susan and said, "My dear Susan, you have truly been like a mother to me this past year. I so admire you. Thank you for all you have taught me and for bringing me here today. I will enjoy singing the carols knowing I am carrying on your wonderful tradition."

"You can go next, Maggie. Brendan will be back shortly."

"Thank you, Susan."

Alice could see a choir. She would have enjoyed listening to the carol singing if she hadn't been so focused on watching out for Maggie. There was a large crowd around the singers as people gravitated towards the beautiful harmonies. They had just begun 'Good King Wenceslas' when Alice spotted a hurried figure coming towards her. Could it really be her? Was that Maggie coming towards her? Alice's body flooded with hope as she momentarily held her breath, looking hard at the person approaching the tree. It was. It really was Maggie. The hope spilt over into joy, fear, excitement and anxiety. Alice wasn't sure if her mother had also spotted Maggie as she didn't want to take her eyes off Maggie to look across the road. Alice wanted to run towards her, but she had agreed to meet her secretly behind the tree, so she kept her feet rooted to the spot just like the oak. Her insides were bustling like branches and leaves on a windy day. Finally, she was near enough to embrace.

"Oh, Maggie, my dear friend. How I've missed you." She held her so tightly.

"I've missed you, too, Alice. I'm so sorry I didn't tell you I was leaving," Maggie said in tears.

"Don't be sorry. Are you okay?" Alice asked.

"I don't have long. They'll realise I'm missing. It's so good to see you. I wish I could come home with you now," said Maggie.

"You can. Come with me," said Alice.

"I want to leave, but I need a plan. All my things are back at the commune," said Maggie, crying

"Leave your things. We can replace them," encouraged Alice.

"But I've nowhere to live. I can't go to Mum and Dad's, and I have no money," Maggie said desperately.

"Come live with me," Alice pleaded.

"Your mother will never allow it. She's friends with my parents." Maggie had already considered this option.

"She will," said Alice with conviction.

"How do you know?" questioned Maggie.

"She'd do anything for me. I know because she's here," said Alice.

"Here?" said Maggie.

"Yes, look there. There on that bench over the road." She pointed towards Jilly.

Maggie began to cry big tears as she realised that she could go with them. She was shaking. Alice cried too.

"Please come with me, Maggie. We will look after you," Alice pleaded again, desperation clear in her voice.

"But I have to go back for my photograph of Nancy," Maggie suddenly remembered.

"You have a photograph of Nancy?" asked Alice, surprised.

"Yes, they got it for me," answered Maggie.

"But if you go back, you may not get another chance to leave. Please don't go back."

"But I can't leave it. It's the only connection I have to her."

"I swear I'll help you find her, Maggie. Whatever it takes, we won't stop looking, but you have to come with me now," said Alice with such conviction that Maggie believed her.

Maggie knew Susan would be expecting her back at the stall any minute now. Her heart was pounding wildly. Maybe Alice was right; if she didn't leave now, she may not get another chance. Alice stared straight into her eyes in pure desperation, willing her to make the decision to come with her before it was too late. If Maggie left now, she may well never see her again.

The crowd clapped and cheered as another carol came to an end.

"Please, Maggie. Please, I want to help. I love you. You're my best friend. Let me help you," Alice said as she took hold of one of Maggie's hands and held on tightly.

"Okay," said Maggie.

Alice did not wait any more. She didn't care if Maggie was sure or not; she had said okay and that was all she needed. No further conversation. She couldn't risk Maggie changing her mind. She led Alice over the road towards her mother and waved her hand, signalling for her to come to them quickly, which she did. They walked as fast as they could, as running would have drawn unwanted attention. They didn't look back, not once, until they reached the bus station. Alice checked the time on the giant clock and went to find out how soon they could board a bus. They wanted to be out of here!

Maggie thought Alice's mother might be cross with her for getting herself into trouble, but as she came towards her, she embraced her just like a mother would her own daughter. "Oh, my dear Maggie, how we've missed you. I'm so glad you're safe."

Maggie melted into the hug. She unclenched her jaw, released her shoulder and began sobbing.

"Come on. That's right. You get it all out. You're safe now."

Alice returned. "It goes in ten minutes," she said, breathless.

Maggie stiffened again with anxiety. "They'll probably come here to look for me once they've scoured the market. This is where they would look next."

"Let's hope we're on the bus and on our way by then," said Jilly.

"Yes, and the market is so large and busy, it will take a while to search," Alice said, trying to sound reassuring, but she was really quite anxious herself.

"Let's wait with our backs to the entrance but still here in the public space. Surely, they wouldn't want to make a scene and draw attention to themselves," said Jilly.

Alice agreed, adding, "They won't be looking for three women together. Here, put on my hat, then you'll look different from a distance."

They sat huddled together, all holding hands, a team of fearless women bonded together by circumstance.

"What will happen when we get back to Ingleton?" asked Maggie.

"Now, don't you worry about that, dear. Let's just focus on getting on that bus. Then, we have a whole hour to talk things through before reaching Ingleton. The main thing you need to know is that you are our family now. We will take care of you," said Alice's mother.

"How will I ever repay you?" asked Maggie.

"We will take care of you, and you will take care of us. That's what families do."

The bus arrived, and they boarded as quickly as they could. As the bus left the station without sight of Susan or any other community member, their bodies finally flooded with relief. Each talking in a deep breath and exhaling long and slow.

***

When she learned all this through Maggie's first-hand diary accounts, Jess sat and sobbed. She, too, took a deep breath and sighed with relief. What an amazing friendship, and Alice's relationship with

her mother too. Jess could feel the love and support coming off the pages of the diary.
She rummaged through the bottom drawer of her bedside table and retrieved the Christmas card from Alice and Betty – the one with baby Jesus on the front she had found on one of her first visits to 33 Upper Float Street. She stroked the baby's cheek on the front of the card, now understanding the choice of the Christmas card. She knew Alice was still alive. She had so many unanswered questions and desperately wanted to meet her. Jess had to find her as well as her grandmother. She had to do it for Maggie. She knew that both she and Betty still lived in the Dales. She knew from Maggie's diaries that Alice lived in Ingleton. She had to presume she still lived in the same area as her starting point for the search.

Chapter Seven

Ian and Jasmine were having a weekend away in their campervan. They were staying on a working farm near Cockermouth. They'd been away less than 24 hours and had already called Jess four times to check in on her and Yasmin. They had said she would like it there. The campsite had its own tarn and bird aviary and a view of the mountain range in the distance. Jess was venturing outside her comfort zone today to take Yasmin to a baby and toddler group at the local village hall.

She felt stomacher stomach churn as she approached the doors of the old building and immediately thought about retreating to her place of safety. It was at this exact moment she met Judy.

"Hello, good morning," Judy beamed. She had the biggest brown eyes and the kindest face. "Are you coming in for the baby group? I'm Judy, and this is Jax." She heaved opened the large door and skilfully navigated Jax's pushchair up the two stone stairs. She applied the break once inside and helped Jess in with Yasmin in her pushchair.

"I'm Jess. This is Yasmin."

"It's lovely to meet you both. It's this way. Follow me. How old is Yasmin?" enquired Judy.

"She's eleven months next week," said Jess, following Judy down a warren of corridors, wondering how she would have found her own way.

"Jax was eleven months last week. Just in here," Judy opened the door into a large hall with seats around the edge and numerous toys in the middle. A painting activity was set up on a low table with six tiny red chairs. On the far side, away from the playing area, was a small kitchen where two ladies were busying themselves, preparing snacks for the children who are old enough and making teas and coffees for the tired parents, mainly mums.

Jess followed Judy over to the chairs. They both removed their rucksack changing bags, which contained all the necessary equipment for venturing out with an eleven-month-old baby and placed them on the chairs. It was a relief to put the heavy bag down, and they shared a knowing look. Judy moved a floor play mat over to where they sat and a selection of toys – some that rattled, some that played music, one with buttons that made animals pop up. They placed Yasmin and Jax down on the mat to have a play, and they, too, sat down on the floor, periodically shaking toys that rattle for the babies and pulling funny faces at them.

" It's so nice to sit down, isn't it? I had such an awful pregnancy that I feel like my entire body is still adjusting," said Judy.

"May I ask why?" said Jess.

"Of course, love. I had hyperemesis gravidarum. Have you heard of it?"

"I'm not sure, just remind me."

"So, unfortunately, it's a condition that's desperately underfunded for medical research as it's only something that happens to pregnant women. And not to men, my dear!" she winked at Jess, who smiled back. "It's also misunderstood by men and women alike. As soon as I say it's morning sickness, I hear a torrent of 'Oh yes, my wife was sick every morning during pregnancy, but she still went to work every day' or 'Oh yes, I had bad morning sickness. I was once on the bus, and I had to ask the driver to stop because I needed to be sick, but you just get on with it. Most women feel sick in pregnancy, don't they?' That kind of thing, but now, I tell you for sure, they never had hyperemesis gravidarum because this is not how you would describe it." Jess listened intently. It was nice to have an adult conversation with someone other than Dad or Jasmine.

"Really?" said Jess, genuinely interested to hear more.

"Yes. I would not wish it on my worst enemy. Imagine the worst food poisoning or the most violent sickness bug you've ever had. Now, they usually last up to 48 hours, but imagine it doesn't end, it doesn't get better. You cannot lift your head from your pillow without being sick. You sleep on the bathroom floor for weeks. You're too weak to take a shower or wash your hair. You are literally bedbound with a sick bowl as a constant attachment of yourself. Being sick at least once an hour, every hour, every day and every night. I tell you this, you just want to die to make it stop."

"Oh, my goodness. That's awful. I'm so sorry you had to go through that," said Jess.

"Bless your heart, my dear. I went to my first midwife appointment at about twelve weeks, and she said I should have been in hospital. She couldn't believe the state of me. I had lost over a stone since becoming pregnant."

"And the birth, what was that like?" Jess asked.

"It was long, and Jax was breach, so eventful, but I tell you, I'd do it one hundred times over if the choice was that or the hyperemesis. And honestly, if one more person had said to me it was 'just' morning sickness, I would have slapped them hard around their head."

Both ladies paused and looked at each other, and then a fit of giggles exploded between them.

Jess liked Judy. Judy liked Jess. It was the first time Jess could remember belly laughing for a very long time, and it felt good – a little hit of serotonin.

"Now, my dear, tell me about you," said Judy. It felt so natural for Jess to talk openly to Judy.

"Well, I'm a single mother."

"Okay," Judy nodded, encouraging Jess to continue, showing that her she was listening and that there would be no judgement.

"We split up before I found out I was pregnant, and when I told him, he just ghosted me."

"Idiot," Judy said with disdain. She'd only known Jess for 20 minutes, but she was 100 per cent on her side. Jess liked that.

"And after Yasmin was born, I became ill and had to get my dad and stepmum to move in to help look after me and Yasmin."

She looked at Judy, and although it wasn't funny at all, again, she burst out laughing. It sounded so strange saying it out loud that it had shifted something, and she'd enjoyed laughing with Judy so much that she laughed again, and Judy joined her. Then Jax started to cry, and Yasmin started to cry, which somehow made the situation all the more dire and, therefore, all the funnier.

When the two new friends had caught their breath and wiped their tearful eyes, Jess turned to Judy and said, "Oh, Judy, thank you. I can't remember the last time I laughed so much, and I truly needed to."

"You're so welcome, my friend. Look, the tea and biscuits are out," she responded.

"It would be rude not to have a cup," said Jess.

"Absolutely, my dear, and a biscuit."

"Or two?" Jess smiled.

"Or two," Judy agreed.

They continued chatting over the tea and biscuits.

'I'm going back to work next week," said Judy. "It's only part-time for now, but I'm dreading it. I don't want to leave Jax."

"It's so strange, isn't it? You grow this human inside of you and then have a baby so dependent on you, and everyone's like, 'Oh, when are you back at work?' Like you didn't just become a mother for the first time," said Jess.

"Yes, I now wish I hadn't agreed to go back so soon. I organise trades for new-build houses. I'm sure I'll be fine. I did enjoy it before. It just feels very different now, but I don't know if there's ever a 'right' time to go back."

***

Benjamin was in a meeting about strategic management techniques. He was becoming more frustrated by the minute. He just wanted to go home, switch off, and have space to breathe and think. All he had done for the past year was throw himself into work. It had acted as a placeholder. It had filled up his life and his head so that he didn't have to think about Jess or the baby.

"So, the strategy here, would we all agree, would be to empower the employee by not using the words 'you' or 'your' but with alternative phrases such as Ruben's suggestion, 'the product needs clarification' rather than 'your project needs work'."

"What utter rubbish," muttered Benjamin under his breath.

"Ah, Benjamin, do you have something to add?" Rufus, the leader of this riveting meeting, said.

"No, no. Just processing what you've said. All fascinating stuff," Benjamin responded, trying not to sound sarcastic.

"Okay, thanks for that input, Benjamin. Now, let's move on to the final point."

"Thank the Lord and Alleluia ," Benjamin said in his head. He didn't want to delay the end of this meeting with a further invitation to share his thoughts.

Rufus continued. "The final point to cover today is how to collaborate with employees in the workplace by holding pacey bi-weekly one-to-one meetings that won't interrupt employees' productivity and work output. We all know that person who would happily talk to you all day rather than return to work, so we need to move them on and keep to the point in an efficient, methodical way. However, we need to keep in mind that the whole point of this process is for the employee to feel autonomy over their work environment, so we don't want to make them feel rushed or for us as managers to come across as dismissive."

The truth was that Benjamin didn't feel like he had any autonomy over any aspect of his life, so how could he empower his employees to feel like they had any? What he gleaned from the course was that, ultimately, employees get told what to do. However, employees work better if they feel fulfilled. Rather than pay them more or give them incentives, we are going to spend all this time and money training managers in the skill of creating the illusion that each employee has a part in the decision-making of their duties, their input, their roles, when they take their holidays, etc., when in reality, they do not have autonomy over any of these aspects. Let's always make them feel we are doing them a favour, and then they will feel eternally grateful to us and to the company. As a result, they will be more productive by the process of psychological manipulation.

"Can anyone suggest how we keep the one-to-one meeting brief, on task, and yet still make it feel collaborative? "asked Rufus.

Mo put his hand up. "Here we go," thought Benjamin. Mr Know-It-All is going to give the longest verbal diarrhoea answer, and we'll be here for another hour. He couldn't keep a one-to-one meeting pacey or collaborative if he tried, he loves the sound of his own voice too much. Why must we go through this charade?' Benjamin was slowly losing the will to live. He could no longer follow the meeting. He had mentally checked out. He should have been home an hour ago.

Recently, work was no longer acting as a distraction from the thoughts lurking in the shadows of his mind. He hadn't gotten over the fact that Jess had left him. He now realised that his true feelings about Jess having a baby were in stark contrast to the actions he took or rather didn't take when he found out Jess was pregnant. He was so busy trying to prove he could live a happy life without Jess that this had been the anteriority of his thought process and his main goal. Finding out Jess was having his baby messed with this. How could he distance himself from Jess, create a life without her if they were going to have a baby together? This just did not translate in his mind at the time. Therefore, inaction became the way forward. And that had been fine until now, dismissing Jess and the pregnancy from his conscious reality. But now he felt differently. Jess and the baby were now at the forefront of his mind. They were the first thing he thought of when he woke in the morning and the last thing he thought of before closing his eyes at the end of each day. He told himself that he was too late to try to be part of the baby's life now, that it would be too complicated. That Jess wouldn't allow him to be. That he wouldn't be able to bond with the baby, who he had estimated would be around 11 months old by now.

He snapped out of his thoughts back to the present moment when he heard Rufus say, "And that brings us to the conclusion of the meeting. Thank you very much, everyone. Good night." Benjamin made his way home. He unlocked the door, turned off the alarm, and placed his coat and shoes on the stands in the hallway. Silence. He still hadn't got used to living here alone. This was the house he had bought with Jess. He closed his eyes and remembered the day they got the keys. They were so young and in love. It was such an exciting time. They laughed as Benjamin had carried Jess across the threshold. Once inside, they ran excitedly in and out of every room, cheering, "This is our house! This is ours." He could hear Jess laughing, and see her smiling and jumping around, but as soon as he opened his eyes, the sounds faded, and the image distorted.

How had it gone from that memory to him now standing alone in the hallway, with Jess living elsewhere in her own home with his child, who he had never met. He hadn't been there for the pregnancy; he hadn't picked out a car seat or a pram or a cot. He'd not gone out at midnight to get Jess all the food she craved. He hadn't been at the birth or changed a nappy. He dropped to his knees. How could this be true? How could this have happened? How did he get here? He lay on the cold, tiled floor and cried like a wounded animal. How could he ever make this right? He couldn't wind the clock back. He couldn't get back what he had missed. He couldn't give what he should have given. How had he got it so wrong? Maybe Jess and the baby would be better off without him anyway.

Chapter Eight

10 December 1961

I'm sharing a room with Alice. Alice's mum marched across the street to Mum and Dad's house and informed them that I was safe and would need my bed and any clothing I had left behind. Alice's mum said they were stunned into silence and nodded in agreement to everything she requested. She told them she would send over Jimmy and Peter after work to collect everything and have it ready. When I asked how Mum and Dad had responded to me being home after a year of being missing, Alice's mum said she'd not given them the opportunity to respond. She told them not to come over straight away and that I would make the approach if and when I was ready. Jilly had also added that she knew about their granddaughter, Nancy, and they should be disappointed with themselves and how they had handled the situation. She had then left without waiting for any further response, questions or objections.
She and Alice and Alice's dad, Jimmy, have made me feel safe, protected. I won't leave the house yet.

It feels very strange to be back. Tonight, I will be sleeping in my very own bed but not in my home.

Jess turned the page, but that was it. There were no more entries in Maggie's diary. She felt relieved that Maggie went home with Alice but yearned to know more. How did Maggie get on when she was home? Did she speak to her parents again? Did she ever have any more children? How did she end up living here at 33 Upper Float Road? Maggie would feel lost not having Maggie's company to become invested in and take her away from her own very different motherhood battles.

She placed the diary on her bedside table and switched off the lamp. "Goodnight, Maggie," she whispered.

Jess was playing with Yasmin on a sandy beach. It was a beautiful day – a bright blue sky with wispy white clouds scattered around it like a painting. The sea was gleaming and sparkling in the sunlight. Jess felt so peaceful with the sound of the waves rolling in and out. She stood up to take in the view. The warm sun on her back soothed her body and mind. It felt so good. She breathed in the fresh sea air. As she looked down at Yasmin, the sand began to rise, twisting around them in a vortex. Gentle at first, but then wildly. The sand vortex suddenly changed direction and plummeted into the ground opening up a sink hole as the ground disappeared beneath them both. She desperately tried to grab hold of Yasmin. As she grabbed her hands filled with grains of sand which passed through her fingers. As the ground swallowed them both she caught a glimpse of the sky which has turned black. She and Yasmin are now part of the vortex reduced to molecules on sand swirling wildly. Jess thrashes about in her bed eventually waking herself up. Her heart is beating wildly. She is sweating profusely, she is disorientated. Her vision is fussy as she throws off the covers and tries to stare at a single spot on the ceiling while she calms herself. She can here Yasmin crying so she steadies herself, sitting up in the bed and swinging her legs out of the bed and planting her feet on the floor to give her a little balance. She went into the nursery and leaned into the cot placing her hand gently on Yasmin. "Shh shh darling, Mummy's here." Jess' head is dripping with sweat. She wipes her brow with the back of her hand as she checks the time on her phone 4 am. She felt nauseous. Jess wondered if she'd be able to settle Yasmin back to sleep or if this was the start of her day. Since starting the pill she didn't know if she was coming or going with her symptoms fluctuating daily. At least when she was tracking her cycle she could make some sense of it all. She was willing to try anything at this stage though so she was going to stick with the doctors advice. She started to sing to Yasmin an old Irish lullaby that her father had taught her. One that her mother had sung to her.

"Go to sleep my baby

Close your pretty eyes
Angels up above you
Peeping at you dearly from the skies
Great big moon is shining
Stars begin to peek
Time for little dreamy babies
To go to sleep
Little dreamy babies, go to sleep
Go to sleep my baby
Close your pretty eyes
Angels up above you
Peeping at you dearly from the skies
Great big moon is shining
Stars begin to peek
Time for little dreamy babies
To go to sleep
Little dreamy babies, go to sleep"

As she sang, she looked at her phone. Her dad and Yasmin were back later today. They said they'd be home around lunchtime. Eight hours to go thought Jess. She had to hold it together for eight more hours. She could do it she told herself half heartedly. She cried while she sang. She so desperately wanted to go back to sleep.

Jess noticed she had received a message. It says re Peggy Lee. She read this message.

Hello my name is Noah I believe I can help with your family research . I am writing on behalf of my mother. She'd be very interested in talking to you. She know a Peggy Lee for many years and she wonders if it could be the same Peggy Lee that you are looking for? Regards.

Later that day Ian and Jasmin arrived home. Not a moment too soon. Ian was concerned on setting eyes on Jess she looked so pale and tired. He didn't want to make a fuss but he quickly read the situation. "You get yourself off for a nap love. We'll take over from here."

"It's okay Dad, tell me all about the Lake District. Did you have a nice time."

"Yes but we missed this one," said Jasmin scooping up Yasmin for a cuddle.

"Give us an hour or two to settle in, unpack, play with Yasmin, then we'll all sit down for something to eat together and we'll tell you all about it," says Ian. "You get yourself upto bed for a bit."

"Okay Dad. Thanks. I think I will. I've been awake since 4am."

Later they sat down for tea. Ian had made toad in the hole, pork sausages oven baked in a yorkshire pudding batter with onion gravy, mash potatoes and peas. Jess felt a bit more human after a couple of hours sleep and the smell drew her down to the kitchen as her tummy grumbled.

"Dad this smells amazing," she said.

"Well you know I like to cook in this swanky new kitchen. And there's nothing better than a proper home cooked meal and not a microwave dinner." Which he knew would have been what Jess had been eating whilst they were away.

"I have had a lot of microwave meals recently." Said Jess.

Ian wrapped an arm around her. A spatula in the other hand that he was using to stir the gravy.

"Now then shall we get the table set and this dished up?"
He called Yasmin and Jas in from the front room.
"This smells amazing. I'm so hungry," said Jas putting Yasmin in her high chair.
"Did you manage to nod off, love?" she asked Jess putting her arms around her. It made Jess feel safe.
"Yes thank you. I felt awful before. I'm still tired but I feel more with it," she responded.
"Well were here tonight.. If this little one decides to be wide awake in the middle of the night," she said wiggling Yasmin's toes and making her laugh.
They sat down and began to eat.
" Did you have a nice time, then?"
"Yes, it was a lovely campsite, beautiful views," answered Jas.
"And the local pub served a good pint," added Ian.
"The weather wasn't bad either," said Jas.
"Did we miss anything here?" asked Ian.
It was then that Jess remembered the message she'd received. She stood up from the table to pick her phone up from the kitchen work top. "Ah well actually that reminds me. I had a message last night about finding Grandma. Let me read it to you. I was so tired when I saw it that I had totally forgotten. Jess read Noah's message to her dad and Jasmine.
After taking it all in, Ian responded, "Well, I suppose we ought to reply, then. What shall we say?"

"How about: 'Thank you for your message. The Peggy Lee I am looking for would probably be in her 80s. Would this fit with the Peggy your mum knows? I would love to chat to your mum to find out more.'" suggested Jas.

"Do you think that's enough information for now? Or do you think we should ask if this Peggy Lee gave up a daughter for adoption?" said Ian.

"I think maybe it is enough for now. We don't want to ask too many questions until we are sure we're not going to scare off our only lead. If Noah's mum is willing to talk to us, let's go with it, I guess."

Jess typed out the message as Jas had suggested and pressed send.

Over the next few days, Jess and Noah exchanged the following messages.

"Hi Jess. Yes, my mum is 84, and her friend Peggy is the same age. Would you like to meet up in person or speak on the phone? My mum is happy to do either, depending on where you're based. If you are near enough, you could meet Mum somewhere close to her house. Can I ask what your family connection to Peggy is?'

"Hi Noah. So, the Peggy I am looking for would be my maternal grandmother. I'll pass on my phone number to you, and then, if you'd be kind enough to pass it on to your mother, she could ring me? Or I'm happy to take her number and ring her."

Noah had gone off line...

LATER THAT DAY

"Jess, my mum said to give you her number. She said, please ring her whenever is convenient for you. She is looking forward to your call."

Ian and Jas had taken Yasmin out for the day, so Jess made the call before she had too much time to think about it.
Ring, ring
Jess takes a sharp inhale.
Ring, ring
Jess thinks about hanging up.
"Hello," an elderly lady answers the phone.
"Hello," says Jess, realising she had never asked Noah for his mother's name. "I hope you don't mind me calling. Noah gave me your number. I'm Jess."
"Hello, Jess. I'm thrilled you called. You are looking for information on a lady called Peggy Lee?" she said.
"Yes, I am looking for a Peggy Lee, who I believe is my maternal grandmother. I'm afraid I only have a little information based on what my mother and father passed on to me. But maybe if it is the same Peggy, we may be able to unravel a bit more about her."
"Of course, dear. My Peggy is a dear friend. We grew up together, even lived together for a few years. And she did have a daughter."
"Okay, so if it is the same Peggy, that daughter would have been my mother."

"Was your mother adopted, my dear?" asked the lady.

"Yes, she was, and I know my adoptive grandparents but never thought to look for my mum's biological mother. Well, not until I became a mother myself," explained Jess.

"You're a mother. How lovely."

"Yes, I have a little girl called Yasmin. She's nearly one."

"Oh, that's just wonderful," said the lady.

Jess relaxed. They talked with ease, not like strangers.

"So, Peggy became pregnant at 20, which was in 1960. What year was your mother born?"

"1960," said Jess as she shuddered, thinking this could be it. This lady might know where my grandmother is. "Can you tell me anything else?"

"Yes, she had the baby at a mother and baby home in some rural spot in the Yorkshire Dales. Now, if only I could remember the name of it. It's been many years, dear. My memory is not as sharp as it once was. It was a Catholic place with nuns. Awful to her, they were. Saint... Saint…"

"Saint Boniface?" said Jess.

'Yes, Saint Boniface. How did you know?"

"That's one of the few pieces of the jigsaw we have. I know that my mother was adopted from Saint Boniface from some information my grandparents passed on to her many years ago. It must be, then, mustn't it? Your friend is my grandmother. Where can I find her?"

"Well, I haven't seen her for a few years, but I have her address if you'd like it. I'll just get it for you."

There was silence for a few minutes, and Jess began to feel excited at the prospect of meeting her grandmother, her mother's mother.

The lady came back to the phone.

"Right, dear, are you ready? Do you have a pen?' said the lady.

"Yes, I'm ready when you are."

"Right then. It's 33 Upper Float Road, West Yorkshire."

"I'm sorry. Can you repeat that?" said Jess, not quite believing what she had just heard.

"That's 33 Upper Float Road, West Yorkshire. Do you want the postcode?" said the lady.

"No, no. I know the postcode," said Jess.

"You do?" The lady was confused.

There was silence for a moment.

"Are you still there, dear?"

"Yes. I'm just a little confused. Your friend is called Peggy?"

"Yes, but no one ever called her that. She's known as Maggie."

"Maggie?"

"Yes, Maggie, dear. Are you okay?"

"So, your friend Maggie lives at 33 Upper Float Road?"

"Yes."

"Your friend Maggie gave up a baby when she was 20 at Saint Boniface mother and baby home?"

"Yes."

"And… I'm sorry, but your son never told me your name."

"I'm Alice."

Jess's heart beat wildly. Her hands were shaking, and she felt tears building and forcing their way out. She cried. Then she laughed. Then she cried again. This wasn't real. It couldn't be. She couldn't be talking to Alice. The Alice who had rescued Maggie from the Community. Alice, the best friend of the lady who had lived in her house. Who had left her diaries for Jess to find.

"Did Maggie call her baby Nancy?"

"Nancy. Yes. But they'd have changed it, you know, because it was the adoptive parents who got to name the child, not the birth mother. So, I imagine your mother wasn't brought up as Nancy, was she?

"No, Elizabeth."

"Aw, well, that's a fine name too. I can't believe I've finally found her after all these years. Is she well, your mother?"

Jess's heart sank. Of course, Alice had promised Maggie she'd find Nancy back when she rescued her all those decades ago. Alice thought both Maggie and Nancy (Elizabeth) were alive. Jess couldn't bring herself to tell her over the telephone. Besides, how could she possibly explain everything when she was in so much shock herself? So, instead, she arranged to meet Alice in person.

The agreed local cafe was just a stone's throw away from Alice's home. Jess asked if it was OK to bring her dad and suggested that Alice might bring Noah. She wanted Alice to have someone there for support when she had to break the news of the death of her beloved friend and that her mother was no longer here either.

Jess, Ian, Jas and Yasmin all set off for their day out to the Yorkshire Dales. Jas would take Yasmin to a park and maybe look around some shops while Ian and Jess met Alice and Noah. Ingleton was nice. Smaller than Jess had imagined. A handful of gift shops, several cafes, and a fish and chip shop. There was one little grocery store and three pubs. There were beautiful walks in the countryside, one leading to a stream. She could imagine Maggie, Alice and Betty dancing in that stream. She wondered if it had changed much in the past 60 years.

They parked in the main car park. Jess and Ian said goodbye to Jas and Yasmin and set off for the short walk to the café, Cobblers, where they had arranged to meet. They were first to arrive, so they found a table for four by the window and ordered a pot of tea. They were both pretty nervous. On the way, they had discussed who would tell Alice the news. Though very nervous, Jess thought it should be her that told Alice. She had built a rapport with her on the phone, and she felt like she knew her in part because of reading about her in Maggie's diaries.

As they entered, Jess somehow knew it was Alice straight away. She had green eyes that sparkled with the wisdom of a life well lived. They still looked young despite the ageing, wrinkled skin that surrounded them. She had thinning white hair and the kindest smile. She'd clearly dressed up for the occasion. She wore a blue blouse and a navy skirt, flat, comfortable shoes that were pink and a beautiful pink silk scarf to match. Her walking stick was also pink, which made Jess smile as she thought of the saying, "Youth is wasted on the young." Alice was accompanied by a man in his late 50s, equally stylish, with a grey beard and wearing a pristine white shirt, leather waistcoat, dark blue jeans and black polished shoes.

Jess stood to greet them, and Alice embraced her like a long-lost daughter. It was a special moment for both of them. Eventually, they sat. After the introductions, Ian ordered another pot of tea for everyone.

"I can't believe I'm looking at Maggie's granddaughter after all these years. It takes my breath away how much you look like her," said Alice.

"Really?" said Jess, not quite comprehending how she was now part of the living story straight out of the pages of Maggie's diary.

"I still can't quite believe this," said Alice.

"Us too," said Ian, "it's an absolute pleasure to meet you."

"You said you had more to tell us?" said Noah.

"Ah, yes. Where to begin?" Jess questioned herself. Ian gave her an encouraging nod.

"Well, first of all, I must tell you that my mother died when I was a baby."

"Oh, my dear, I'm so sorry. Dear Nancy. Apologies, I mean Elizabeth. I don't mean to be disrespectful."

"I'm so sorry," Noah said politely. "What happened? If I may ask?"

Ian took this question, and Jess appreciated that. She was so glad they'd come together.

"We think she had a chronic illness called Premenstrual Dysphoric Disorder, which was somehow exacerbated giving birth. Unfortunately, it was undiagnosed at the time, and this led to severe depression. Very sadly, she took her own life."

Alice was upset by this revelation. Though she'd never met Elizabeth, she felt a connection to her, as she had spent so many years searching for her, continuing even when Maggie herself gave up.

"Are you okay, Mum?" asked Noah.

"Yes, yes." Alice waved her hand dismissively. "Don't be worried about me. I'm just sorry for your loss. She looked at Ian and then Jess. Growing up without a mother."

"Oh no, I have a wonderful mother in my stepmother Jas. She's here somewhere, actually. She came with us. She's looking after Yasmin," said Jess, smiling, thinking of her little daughter.

"Yasmin. That's your little one," Alice said as that warm smile. "Will I get to meet her?"

"I'm sure we can arrange that," said Jess, feeling bad that she had more bad news to share with Alice. Now that she was here, she wasn't actually sure that it was the right thing to do, but she could hardly let her go on not knowing what happened to her dear best friend Maggie. Surely, it was best to come from Jess, she was her granddaughter after all. She felt it was her responsibility but didn't want t to hurt her.

"Will you go see Maggie? She'd be happy to see you. I know she would."

"Well, I have been getting to know Maggie, in an unexpected way," said Jess. She leaned into her bag and produced Maggie's diary and Alice's Christmas card.

"First, I have to be the bearer of some very said news. I'm so sorry, but Maggie passed away about a year and a half ago," Jess said.

There was a brief silence. Noah placed his hand on his mother's for a moment. Then Alice spoke.

"Deep in my heart, I think I knew. When she stopped sending birthday cards and Christmas cards. We're not getting any younger, are we? I just hoped that they'd got lost in the post. I thought if I kept sending my cards, it was like keeping her alive." A tear rolled down her cheek, and she quickly wiped it away.

"Well, here's the end of the sad news and the beginning of an unbelievable story," said Jess. Alice and Noah sat to attention, both utterly intrigued. Jess told them about how she had first come to Maggie's house and how she ended up buying it. Then, she told them about finding the diary.

Noah invited everyone to his house as it was clear this was going to be a longer conversation than he had ever imagined, and Alice was becoming uncomfortable on the wooden chair. "We'll go ahead, and I'll get Mum comfortable. You track down Jas and little Yasmin. I'll send you the directions, and we'll see you shortly."

Benjamin pulled up in his car outside Jess's house. It was the first time he had been here. He wished he'd paid more attention when she was selling it; then, he could at least have created a mental picture about where Jess and his baby were living. Instead, he had a blank screen whenever he tried to picture them, which made him feel more detached. He could see Ian and Jasmine's classic 1967 VW T1 Split-Screen campervan in cream sitting on Jess's driveway. He hadn't known they were back. He supposed they must be visiting Jess and their grandchild. Benjamin didn't even know if Jess had had a boy or a girl. If he had a son or a daughter. He had cut off every tie to Jess, including closing down his social media accounts. He never really used them anyway. Seeing the camper made him nervous. He had to prepare to face Jess's father too. What he imagined he might have to say to him made his toes curl. But given the low hedge, the wide front window, and the fact that he had stupidly parked right outside, he presumed that he or his car would have been spotted by now. He'd come this far. He took a deep breath, gathered himself for a moment and prepared himself for what he expected to be a negative reception from whoever would open the door. He walked up the path, admiring the flowers in the front garden. He hadn't realised Jess was into gardening.

There were new stairs up to the door, and all the way down the side of them in concrete were the initials J&Y. He puzzled over the significance. J for Jess, perhaps, but who was Y? He was standing at the front door now and couldn't see anyone through the front window. He moved his head closer towards the door, turning his ear so it almost touched the glass pane. He listened. It was quiet. Maybe nobody was home. There was no doorbell, so he knocked politely and waited. He shook his hands and jumped a little hop on the top step like you see boxers do when psyching themselves up for a big match. Adrenaline flooded through his body. He knocked again, this time much louder. Again, he waited. Nothing. He knocked one final time for good measure to be sure no one was home.

He peered in through the window this time. He could see a cosy front room with a cast-iron gas fire in a stone surround and a chunky wooden beam mantle. A fireguard surrounded it. He imagined that the baby was on the move now, crawling, shuffling, maybe even walking. There were a few toys scattered about the floor. On one of the two two-seater sofas was a bag of nappies. He finally had a small glimpse into a life that wasn't his but a life that might have been. This was the closest connection he had had to his child. He turned away from the window, returned to his car and drove away.

Chapter 9

They were all made very welcome back at Noah's place. His wife Amy had quickly put together an impressive buffet of ham sandwiches cut into triangles, cheese and pineapple on cocktail sticks, a salad of lettuce, tomatoes and cucumber, a cheese and broccoli quiche, biscuits, and a carrot cake. She kept apologising that it wasn't much, and if she'd known they were coming, she would have baked scones.
"It's all lovely," said Jas.
"Oh, yes," said Ian in agreement as he reached for his second ham sandwich.
"Thank you," said Jess, Yasmin bouncing and wriggling on her knee, enjoying a biscuit.
Once everyone had settled down in the living room, all eyes turned to Jess to continue with her story.
"So, as I was saying, there has been an unbelievable connection between Maggie and me, though we never met. It seems fate wanted me to

know her, and a series of events led me to her, though I did not know at this point she was actually my grandmother."

No one interrupted; they couldn't wait to hear what Jess might reveal next. The only person who made a sound was Yasmin, who bounded along to sit on her grandfather's knee.

"I'm an estate agent, and a property came onto my list. I visited the property to make an evaluation, and that's when I found your Christmas card, Alice. There was no return address, so I took it home and stood it up with my own and that's where it all began, I suppose. The house didn't sell before Christmas that year, and circumstances led me to need a new home, so I bought Maggie's house." Alice and her family gasped with surprise.

"You bought Maggie's house?" Noah said, checking the information he had just heard.

"Yes, yes, we all live there. Me, Dad, Mum" – she smiled at Jas, who was now playing with Yasmin – "and Yasmin."

"Oh, my goodness, this is truly unbelievable," said Amy. "Isn't it, Alice?"

"So, when I read Maggie's address out to you when I spoke to you, that's where I was," continued Jess.

"Right there in Maggie's home? Your home," said Alice.

"Yes." Jess smiled.

"Well, if that doesn't mean something, I don't know what does," said Alice. Noah sat by his mum's side on the arm of her chair. She gently shook his arm, smiling again.

"There's more," said Ian, smiling too.

"More?" Noah looked like he couldn't take much more.

Jess continued. She told them about the diary. She asked about Betty, who she now learned lived in a nursing home. She and Alice still talked regularly on the phone. Alice reminisced and told them about the happier times the three girls had enjoyed together growing up. Jess really wanted to know more about Maggie's later life and how she had come to live in the mountain village, but time was ticking on, and both Yasmin and Alice were getting tired. Jess was, too, so those stories would have to wait for another time. They said their goodbyes and promised to keep in touch. Yasmin fell asleep on the drive home, and Jess managed to put her down in her cot without waking her. It had been a long, eventful and poignant day. Jess went straight to bed, too, and they both slept right through the night for the first time in forever.

The problem with living with a high 'normal' baseline of anxiety is that when life happens, you have little capacity to deal with it without being completely flooded and overwhelmed. You feel guilty for not being able to cope and support others around you as they rightly forget that you're sick and dealing with your own crisis. As you see someone you care for busy dealing with 'life', you try to pick up the pieces to help them, pushing your own requirements to the bottom of the pile – basics like getting a good night's sleep, fresh air, moving your body, eating well. Jess had always tried to be all things to all people. She was overly concerned with what people thought of her when, in reality, their opinion didn't, or at least shouldn't, matter at all.

Ian knew this very well. So, when Benjamin started messaging Jess about how depressed and messed-up he was feeling, Ian was extremely worried that this would upset the status quo and the good routine the four of them – Jess, Yasmin, Jas and himself – now had in place. Jess regularly took Yasmin out for coffee and playdates with Judy and Jax. She'd returned to work two days a week and been referred to a gynaecologist. She had good days and bad, but the general trend was up. Her good routines sustained her. She'd worked so hard to cultivate them, but they could still quickly crumble away if extra stress was added to the mix, and this was exactly what was happening with Benjamin.

Jess had made peace with bringing Yasmin up as a single mother, but now here he was back in their lives, wanting a piece of her. She needed to make the right choices for Yasmin. The whole situation weighed heavy on her. She pushed through daily chores and activities, things that couldn't be put aside to make space for this intrusion into her life. But as ruminating thoughts of Benjamin occupied her mind she stopped socialising, getting out for walks and eating well.

Ian could see Jess slipping away again. The glazed-over eyes, the one-word answers, going straight to bed at the same time as Yasmin without eating a proper meal. Jess knew this was happening, and she berated herself, telling herself she was useless, a failure, childlike, unable to cope. Even though she was coping, she couldn't appreciate this herself. How could she expect others to remember she had a chronic illness if she didn't allow herself to remember, to celebrate everything she was able to cope with despite overwhelm, fatigue, stress and anxiety experienced daily to a level that most people would never endure or understand?

She couldn't just turn off her illness and step up to solve the situation. This was a time that she really needed to be kind to herself. Ian knew she required checking in on more than ever, and she needed the grounding of the good habits she had built to sustain herself at this time. When selflessness is revered as the gold standard in society to being a 'good' woman, her own needs fall way back on her priority list. Jess longed to thrive in her life, not just to survive minute to minute. She wanted not to be entirely consumed by the anxiety but to be able to navigate her way through life and motherhood as a functional person.

Jess sat on the floor in her room in front of a pile of washing, mainly Yasmin's clothing. She had lunch to make and the washing to put in the machine – seemingly small tasks – but she sat frozen to the spot, staring into space. Her body as still as a statue, her mind blustering, with one thought jumping on top of another, leading to all-or-nothing catastrophic thinking, which made everyday tasks seem so irrelevant. But they needed doing.

How could she 'fix' this glitch in her brain? She needed to function now, even at a base level; it was essential to living. Why did her body think that shutting down was helpful? Her mind raced into a future that didn't exist as she concluded she could not cope with hypothetical disastrous situations and losses. She needed to jerk herself into action. She picked up her phone, called Judy, and arranged a road trip to see Alice again.

Judy beeped her horn full of enthusiasm as she arrived outside Jess's house the following Friday morning. It was the first time either of them had left their children since they were born. They were going to the Dales for the weekend. They had intended to book a bed and breakfast, but Alice had insisted they would stay with her. Jess stood in her front room. She waved to Judy from the window.

"So, if you need anything just call me. Even if it's the middle of the night," Jess said to Ian and Jas.

"We'll be fine. Everything will be fine," said Ian.

"Okay. Thanks, Dad."

She hugged them all goodbye, giving Yasmin some extra kisses. Judy beeped again.

"Right. That's me, then. Bye. Love you all."

***

Judy put the kettle on and made the tea. Jess cut up the Victoria sponge they had picked up on the way. She had asked Alice what her favourite was.

She placed the slices on Alice's beautiful china plates adorned with pink peonies. The tea cups matched, and it felt like they had gone out for afternoon tea.

They all settled into the front room, and Alice began to tell the story of what had happened to Maggie once she had returned home.

So, Maggie found it quite difficult to adjust to being home. My mum was amazing with her. She treated her like a second daughter, and she was like a sister to me. We shared a room, and, bit by bit, the light returned to her eyes. Yes, there were moments of sadness, but also laughter and love. We made a lifelong pact to find Nancy, swearing on it no matter how long it took. I just wish she was alive to meet you, my dear. May she rest in peace, never knowing what happened to your dear mother. I think that would have broken her. Though if she's looking down on us today, I know she'll be so happy we found each other. Putting together the pieces of Maggie's and your mother's story is like honouring their lives and bringing it all full circle. And you'll be able to tell your Yasmin about them and me, hopefully," she smiled.

"Absolutely," said Jess.

Alice continued.

"Well, there's a story, my dear, if you're ready to hear it?"

"Oh yes," said Judy.

"Yes," nodded Jess.

My dear mother, God rest her soul, went to a private college to learn shorthand and typing and double-entry bookkeeping. She worked at the local garage doing secretarial work – typing and sending letters, bookkeeping, making cups of tea for the mechanics, whatever they wanted doing. We had a typewriter at home, so Mum trained Maggie. She said that since everyone thought she was qualified for secretarial work, she might as well learn and get a job. "That will show your mother and father," she'd said. Mother had found a way to be rebellious yet always stay within the lines. I loved that about her. They spent every evening for about three months working on Maggie's training. Then Mother announced that there was no more she could teach her. She was fully trained. She even typed out a certificate for Maggie, saying she'd undertaken a training course.

Well, as it happened, a job came up in the village, and as everyone already thought Maggie was more than qualified due to her parents 'lies', no one questioned the certificate my mother had made, and Maggie got the job. She was good at it too. So, she started earning her own money. The best thing was that her parents couldn't discredit her without discrediting themselves.

"Yes, Maggie!" cheered Judy. Jess smiled and turned back to Alice, ready to learn every detail she could tell her. Jess topped up Alice's teacup.

"As for finding Nancy, first we went to the police station and said we'd like to report a missing person, but once we gave the details, they told us

that, as Maggie had signed the adoption papers of her 'own free will', it was not a missing person's case. But we learned that there would be a copy of the adoption paperwork held at Saint Boniface, so Maggie typed out a letter requesting the details of the adoption. She did get a reply, but it just said that as she had agreed to the adoption, it was no longer her concern. We even took a bus ride out there but didn't even get beyond the gates."
"Wow, you both did all that?" said Jess.
"Yes, but unfortunately we never got anywhere."
"Maggie became more confident, more beautiful, as she found success with work and with the love and adoration from myself and my mother. It was so lovely to hear her belly laughing again. She did see her mother once or twice again, but as much as she would have loved a good relationship with her, the bond had been shattered and could not be fixed."

"So, when did she move away? Did she ever have any more children?" asked Jess.
"She was engaged to a man once but never made it down the aisle. Her choice. I think she was too much of a free spirit at that point. She liked living life her way. She didn't want to become a housewife and had no more children. She was amazing with my Noah, though. She was a natural with children.

She moved for work in 1982 when she was 42. Oh, how I missed her, but I was married and had Harold and Noah, so I couldn't ask her to stay for me. After all, she wasn't moving to the other side of the world. She became a doctor's receptionist for a GP surgery. She loved that job. It really suited her. She wrote often. She had lots of new friends. One friend, Mabel, I think she was called, was a keen gardener and spent Sunday afternoons helping Maggie in her garden. Maggie seemed to like that and got rather good at it."

"Yes," said Jess, "I can see that now in my garden. It's beautiful."

"She used to try to help mothers in the same position. She started a support group in the community centre, and they'd share their experiences. She was always surrounded by people, but she lived alone. I guess after losing Nancy, being betrayed by her own parents and then living in the commune, she'd had enough bad experiences to make her think she'd prefer to be alone. She loved helping people, but she didn't want to rely on anybody but herself. I think she was happy, though. I hope she was. I just wish you'd both known her, you and your mother Elizabeth, her daughter. Do you have any pictures of your mother, dear? I'd love to see her," said Alice.

"Oh yes, I brought lots of photographs. Let me show you," said Jess. Judy passed her the folder she'd brought.

"So, this is Mum as a little girl playing hide and seek in the garden with her parents," said Jess. "They all look so happy." Alice put her hand to her face as tears of relief and happiness started to fall.

"Look at this one," said Jess. "Mum's on holiday at the beach here. And here's Mum and Dad on their wedding day."
"I love that one. They look so in love," said Judy.
"And this is me and Mum. I'm about four months old there."
They talked into the evening, and Alice showed Jess and Judy pictures of Maggie. It felt so good to all of them to bring Maggie and her daughter together in their memories. Eventually, Alice fell asleep in her chair, so it was time for bed.
The next morning, the trio sat together for breakfast as the sun streamed in through the window. It was such a peaceful morning.
"Can I ask about Yasmin's father?" enquired Alice.
"Benjamin. We'd recently broken up when I found out I was pregnant. I told him. I gave him quite a few chances to be involved, but he stopped contact with me."
"I'm sorry, my dear," said Alice.
"Well, now, when Yasmin turns one next month, he wants to see her. And I don't know what to do. If I, as the mother, had said I didn't want her and then decided a year later, I do now, it would be too late. But he can do this. He hasn't mentioned solicitors or anything, but he has rights. His name is on the birth certificate."
"He has no right," said Judy, cross.
"And what about Yasmin? He's her father. I would do it for her, not for him. But the idea of him taking her for whole weekends or having to

be without her on special occasions as we 'take turns', oh, I just can't bear it," said Jess.

Judy stood behind Jess to wrap her arms around her, and Alice reached across the table and placed it on top of Jess's hand.

"She needs a happy mother," said Alice. "It's time to be selfish, not selfless, despite what society would have you believe."

Alice's forthrightness quite took Jess and Judy aback, but in a positive way.

Alice continued, "It needs to be on your terms, and the best way to do this is by not working against him but setting clear boundaries. You need to meet with him face-to-face to work out his intentions before considering him meeting Yasmin. Is he in it for the long haul and for the right reasons? Before you meet him, I want you to write a list about what you are and what you are not prepared to accept."

Jess greatly appreciated this advice. It made her feel completely supported. It empowered her.

"Don't disclose yourself," Alice added.

Jess looked confused, waiting for more.

"You must be civil for your own peace of mind, but you're not partners, not friends even. He doesn't need to know about you on a personal level like he used to. Think of him more like a colleague if he becomes a co-parent. If."

"I agree," said Judy. "You have so much on your plate already with your diagnosis and your treatment and coming to terms with the fact that your mother could have been helped too. If he takes this second chance, it must work for you and

Yasmin. Speaking to a solicitor t about where you stand legally sounds like sound advice too."
"Knowledge is power," said Alice.

***

It was 1 pm as Jess walked through the doors of the coffee shop. She was taken aback when she saw Benjamin sitting there; he'd never been on time for anything in his life. Jess felt very uncomfortable. But she'd told herself this was necessary. She wanted to run away, but this problem would only follow her. Benjamin lifted his head when he spotted her and did this awkward "I want to seem friendly, but this is serious, so not too much enthusiasm or happiness behind it" limp wave. Jess made her way towards him. She was going to take control even if she did feel like a tiny mouse going into the lion's den.
"I'm just going to order a coffee. I see you've already got one." Jess went to the counter, worried her assertiveness had come off as rudeness.
"Don't get his back up," she said to herself. "Don't get angry, we're not here to fight. Be assertive and clear. You can do this." She ordered, took a deep breath and went back to the table to sit down.
"You look well," Benjamin said to her.
"Thank you. How have you been?" replied Jess, fidgeting with her fingers under the table, trying to appear calm. Like a graceful swan above the water with its feet and legs paddling furiously underneath.
"Okay, thanks. Thank you for meeting me."

A young man brought Jess's coffee. She smiled and said thank you, but she didn't take a drink because she thought her hands might shake.

"You want to talk about our daughter?"

" My little girl?" said Benjamin.

"She's not so little anymore," said Jess, sounding snappier than she meant to.

"What did you call her?" asked Benjamin.

"Yasmin Elizabeth."

"After your mum and Jas. That's nice."

This was harder than Jess had imagined. He knew so much about her; they had a history. She felt she might cry with frustration that he'd not been there, not just for Yasmin but for her when they were still together.

"Listen, I'm open to you having a relationship with Yasmin. You've missed the pregnancy and the newborn stages as she's nearly one, but at some point, she will want to know her father. How do you see your involvement? What do you think it will look like?"

Benjamin quickly tried to prepare a good answer. He hadn't known what to expect from meeting Jess today, but now he knew. He was being interviewed for the role of 'Dad', and if he didn't get it right, he wouldn't get the job. He also needed to answer quickly so that it didn't seem like he hadn't put enough thought into being a father after having already missed so much.

"Jess, I know I've let you and Yasmin down. I just want a chance to get to know her. To be honest, I thought you'd tell me what that was going to look like, as you're the one bringing her up. You know

what's best for her, but I'm guessing you want her to know me too or else you wouldn't be here."
There was a short silence before Jess spoke again, and Benjamin couldn't gauge her response.
"Okay. We'll meet you at the park on Saturday. Just for one hour. I'll give you the location. I won't allow you to introduce yourself as Daddy at this point in time. Your Mummy's friend, okay?"
"Yes, okay. Thank you," said Benjamin.
Jess finally took a drink of her coffee.
"Benjamin, if you break any of the boundaries I've just laid out, then next time we don't meet at a coffee shop, we meet in my solicitor's office."
She stood up, and Benjamin stood up too. She picked up her handbag and said, "I'll send you a message with the time and the place." With that, she walked out the door, leaving Benjamin standing there, taking in what had just happened.
It wasn't magical, like in the movies, the day that Benjamin met Yasmin. It was the day before her first birthday, on a warm September's day in the little park down the road, with the baby swings, one of which was broken, and the little blue climbing frame with the peeling paint and the metal slide. Benjamin seemed awkward; he didn't know how to interact with an almost-one-year-old. He did try, though, and Jess could tell he really wanted to be there as he'd been early, not late. He stuck to Jess's rules, and when the hour was up, he didn't push for more time. He had introduced himself to Yasmin as Mummy's friend. He made her laugh, but he had a long way to go before becoming "Dad".

Chapter Ten

34 Years Before

It was a cold March evening. Ian had returned home from work to his two girls. They both sat in the gloom, playing with building blocks and watching Thomas the Tank Engine on TV. Elizabeth looked up at him and said,
"Is it okay if I go for a walk? Get some fresh air on my own."
"Of course. I'll just get changed, and then I'll come play with Jess," said Ian.
Ian had gone upstairs to get changed like he usually did. He came back downstairs to see Jess and said, "Bye-bye, see you in a bit. Enjoy your walk," to Elizabeth.
Elizabeth had walked and walked, hoping the wind would blow away the darkness from her mind to clear her thoughts. She walked and walked, not knowing where she was headed.
Elizabeth walked and walked, desperate to run away, but she couldn't run away from her

thoughts. She walked and walked, searching her brain for answers. She walked and walked, wondering if she was not cut out for this life. As her anxiety grew and grew, she could see no future where she would ever feel better. She did not know why she felt this way. She looked at other mothers enjoying life, beautiful mothers in perfect outfits, perfect hair, perfect groups of friends, babies sleeping through the night. She could hardly get dressed some days. She thought she must have been born like this, too sensitive, too weak. There must be a flaw in her. "Maybe that's why your real mother didn't want you," a nasty voice that sounded just like her own told her. "Maybe you weren't meant to be born. It would have been easier to have never been born," more intrusive thoughts told her. "If you're waiting for it to get easier, it won't." The thoughts continued, demonising her mind until she began to believe they were all true. She walked for miles and miles, fearing if she stopped, the darkness would engulf her. She was oblivious to time. It never crossed her mind that Ian would be wondering where she had got to.

She never returned home that night. Ian wished she had run away. Then maybe one day, he could have had her back, but you can't run away from yourself.

At 4 am, the police knocked on the door. Elizabeth's body had been found.

Maggie had been desperate to keep her daughter, Elizabeth, but she had no rights over her own body and over whether she got to keep her own child. She was controlled by societal expectations and finances and forced into the barbaric situation of having to live and work in a mother-and-baby home. Elizabeth's adoptive parents, Rose and Arnold, were unable to have their own children and always felt that they had been blessed with the gift of their daughter. She was one of the lucky ones as she had a good upbringing and was loved unconditionally. Ian also loved Elizabeth, and they married and started a family. They had their beautiful baby girl, Jess. Illness isn't logical; intrusive thoughts tell us lies masquerading as truth. Anxiety and depression destroy. Ian had vowed that day, the day he lost Elizabeth, to protect his little girl. And now he had a granddaughter too. He was going to do everything and anything he could, as Jess was, to advocate for women's health – especially women's menstrual and mental health, which are so taboo. Jess agreed to participate in medical research. She filled out questionnaires, was interviewed, and agreed to try hypnotherapy, emotional freedom techniques, reflexology, yoga, supplementation, seed cycling, and counselling. You name it, Jess tried it. She wanted things to be different for Yasmin. She documented her whole experience on social media to raise awareness and help other women.

Jess was asked to speak at an Every Women Matters event. As she waited backstage, she jigged up and down on the spot, trying to shake out her nerves. She listened to Professor Sims, who was currently on stage.

"Why is this the case? It's called 'sexism'. We live in a sexist, patriarchal society. Women are raised from birth to expect to take on the bulk of childcare. Conversely, the majority of boys are raised from birth to expect women to take on the bulk of childcare. This is still happening today; it's woven into societal expectations. This sexist cultural view then influences employer decisions not to hire mothers, not to promote mothers, to sack pregnant women, and so on. Yeah, we have laws to give lip service to equality, but it's men who make these laws, and sexism has not gone away." Professor Sims received a massive round of applause. Then, it was Jess's turn.

"Our next speaker is Jess Briar. Let's give her a warm welcome to the stage."

Jess couldn't quite believe she was about to speak to a packed audience on this stage.

"Thank you, thank you. I'm Jess Briar. I'm a women's health advocate, and I'm here today to talk about the gender gap in healthcare.

"It may surprise you to learn that the UK healthcare system has been designed around the needs of just half the population. Men have historically been treated as the default patient in clinical practice and medical research, and women's health and healthcare needs have been marginalised. Improved healthcare for women requires change in several areas. The education of healthcare professionals is important, but so are changes in societal attitudes that are shown in stigmatisation and paternalism and a continuing reluctance to ensure that women's needs are addressed in biomedical research and development. Finally, adequate funding is essential to improve women's health and healthcare. In the UK, funding for sexual and reproductive health services has declined, particularly in recent years, resulting in reduced access to services, especially for the most vulnerable women.

"One of those underfunded and under-researched disorders is one that both my mother and myself have suffered from, and that is PMDD. What is PMDD? Premenstrual Dysphoric Disorder is a cyclical, hormone-based mood disorder with symptoms arising during the premenstrual or luteal phase of the menstrual cycle and subsiding within a few days of menstruation. It affects an estimated 5.5 per cent of women and AFAB – assigned female at birth – individuals of reproductive age. While PMDD is directly connected to the menstrual cycle, it is not a hormone imbalance. PMDD is a severe negative reaction in the brain to the natural rise and fall of estrogen and progesterone. PMDD is believed to be heritable, as shown in studies on families and twins. PMDD can cause severe emotional, professional, and personal harm to those who have it.

"There is hope, though, and growing awareness and treatment options. If you would like further information or have any questions you'd like to ask me, please come and find me in the red tent left of the stage. Thank you for your time. Enjoy your day," Jess finished and left the stage to a round of applause.

She found Judy. "Was that okay? Did I remember everything? What did you think? Did Yasmin see me?"

"You were amazing. Yes, Yasmin saw you. She's waiting with Ian and Jas in the red tent. I think they might have some fairy cakes to celebrate," said Judy.

"It's your turn next. Are you ready?" Jess asked Judy.

"Born ready."

Jess stood in the wings listening to her best friend and could not have been prouder as Judy came to the end of her speech.

"So, remember, every year, millions of women across the globe experience great trauma, financial strain, debility and incredible isolation and misery due to hyperemesis gravidarum. Come and find me in the red tent for further information. Thank you."

Chapter Eleven

It was Yasmin's third birthday. Everyone important to her was there: Mummy, Grandad, Grandma, Judy, her husband Austin, Jax, Alice who had become like a great grandmother, Noah and his wife Amy. It was a beautiful September day in the Yorkshire Dales. Alice's garden was long and straight and lush, like a bowling green. Beautiful flowers bloomed around the two longest edges. Noah's wife Amy had put together a magnificent birthday spread, having had plenty of notice this time. She'd baked quiches, scones, fairy cakes and sausage rolls and prepared a fresh, colourful salad, finger sandwiches (especially for the birthday girl), and a jug of orange juice with ice to keep it cool.
Yasmin was toddling around the garden with Jax. They were chasing the bubbles Jaz was blowing for them. A cooling breeze blew in the warm sunshine, and the garden provided enough shaded spots to enjoy. Alice's favourite 60s music

was playing. Jess felt calm, relaxed, safe, supported, and happy. Everyone was having a good time.

Jax and Yasmin were chasing each other down the lawn when Yasmin looked up and called excitedly, "Daddy." He picked her up and smothered her in kisses as she giggled.

He had just popped out to collect the birthday cake he and Jess had ordered from the local bakery. Yasmin had wanted a racing car and a rainbow unicorn. This had made him and Jess snort with laugher, but his baby girl's wish was his command. He left the cake in the kitchen but couldn't wait to see her face when it was revealed to her later.

"Did you get it?" Alice winked at him.

"Sure did. She'll love it," he said.

"Great job, Michael," she said.

Jess came over excitedly.

"What's it like?" she asked Michael.

"It's perfect," he said, hugging her.

"Have you got your outfit for our wedding yet, Alice?" asked Michael. "We are so glad you are coming. If there's anything you need, please let us know."

"You're already getting married in the church on my street so that I can come. I'm sure that's quite enough," Alice smiled.

"Just checking," said Michael.

"Tell me again how you met my beautiful Jess," Alice said to him.

"Again?" said Michael.

"Yes, again. I love to hear it."

Jess laughed. Alice asked Michael every time they visited.

"Well, my dear Alice, a beautiful lady who lives at 33 Upper Float Road, decided to start a business with her best friend Judy – buying and selling houses. The first property they purchased together required some renovation. I had previously worked for Judy, and she asked me for a quote to plaster and paint the entire property. As I arrived at the house to start work, there was a beautiful, mysterious lady" – he nodded toward Jess, whose face lit up as she smiled – "who was having a semi-heated conversation with Judy. It sounded like she was insisting that she didn't need a man to help her with the plastering and painting and that she'd be just fine doing it herself."

Alice laughed at this. "That's my Jess."

"They seemed to come to some sort of agreement, and I was allowed to start work accompanied by said beautiful and mysterious, slightly agitated woman. It took us just over two weeks working side by side to realise we quite liked each other and, more importantly, that my plastering was as smooth as a baby's bottom and worth paying for. Though she had initially worked alongside me to learn how to plaster and never needed my services again, it turned out that we would see each other again. And the rest, as they say, is history."

"Will you tell that one at the wedding?" said Alice, clapping her hands together and smiling.

"I'm sure there'll be some version of it," Jess laughed.

Benjamin had met with Jess and Yasmin twice after the first meeting in the park. He had figured out that all he'd really wanted was to ease his consciousness and not actually be a dad because it was not that easy and he didn't want to dedicate his time to it, so he had sent Jess a message:

"Jess, I feel that you and Yasmin are so strong as a unit of two, and I don't want to come between you. I have been offered a promotion for which I've worked so hard over the years. It's a position in America. I'll be there for six months initially, so maybe I can get in touch when I get back. Take care, Benjamin."

She hadn't heard from him since. She had thought it would be just the two of them, Jess and Yasmin. She was happy with that too. Even when she first started dating Michael, she couldn't have imagined marrying him and Yasmin so adoring of him. She was at an age where she saw the other children's daddies picking them up from nursery or pushing them on a swing in the park, and she was so proud to have her daddy. Jess didn't need Michael, but she wanted him. He offered her love and companionship. He was her gentle company. Always there rooting for her. Michael knew from day one that Jess planned to have a full hysterectomy, including the removal of her ovaries. Jess wanted him to have the opportunity to back out of the relationship early doors, as he would never be able to have his own children with her. But Michael didn't see it that way at all. He knew that being a father meant showing up, doing the work, being there; his two girls, Jess and Yasmin, were his world. He wasn't there at Yasmin's birth, but he would be there for every birthday, every Christmas, every school assembly, sports day, and music lesson. He had been there at the hospital when Jess had come round from her hysterectomy surgery, and he would be there for everything.

It was time for the cake, and everyone gathered around the table. Jess and Michael carried the racing car unicorn cake outside, candles lit, Ian ready to video and Jas next to Yasmin.

"Happy Birthday to you, Happy Birthday to you, Happy Birthday, dear Yasmin, Happy Birthday to you."

Printed in Great Britain
by Amazon